Originally from Kent, .eer ...s ... graduating from universi çо ... croupier, and now works as ... ... station. *Everybody Knows This Is N* ... er first novel.

Everybody Knows
This Is
NOWHERE

Alice Furse

Burning Eye

This edition published by Burning Eye Books 2014

www.burningeye.co.uk

@burningeye

Burning Eye Books
15 West Hill, Portishead, BS20 6LG

ISBN 978 1 90913 644 1

For Rob

The Traffic Warden

I always woke up at his alarm.

I'd get breakfast while he was in the shower, and then sit in bed eating sugary cereal – the kind that my mum would never allow – and watch him opening drawers with a towel around his waist. Before he was dry all his hairs pointed downwards, straight as arrows and flowing in the same direction, like trees on a map.

I liked watching him dress. I liked the shapes he made as he put his traffic warden uniform on, as if he was dancing for me. The groove down his bare back as he bent over his belt buckle. The cat-like stretch to tuck his shirt in. I admired the way he remained so scruffy, even with epaulettes.

After he went to work, I would get up and make the bed.

His mum had chosen the duvet some time before I moved in, dark brown with little silky white swirls like sugar decorations embroidered at regular intervals, so it looked more like a huge square chocolate cake than a bed. The pillows matched, and when I lay down they crackled like crepe paper. They felt unused. They felt like guest pillows.

I found his dirty boxers on the bathroom floor almost every morning, usually in a figure of eight where he'd stepped straight out of them.

I'd hook the elastic waistband – slack, grey, peppered with bobbles – on a bent finger, drop them on his pillow, and shut the bedroom door.

I'd open the blinds in the front room and then the windows to let the previous night's smoke out, and then do the washing-up. There were trees outside the window and I watched them sway in the air.

I watched Jeremy Kyle and hated it, made toasted cheese sandwiches and collected second-hand books. I had been led to believe that such a lifestyle would be romantic and bohemian, but it was neither. I batted around the flat with no more clue than a wasp at a window.

I kept rereading a story by Roald Dahl called *The Hitchhiker*, about a man who could take your watch or belt without you knowing. My dad read it to me when I was little, and I had been haunted by it ever since. I don't believe in ghosts but I know you can be haunted.

Every Tuesday I bought the local jobs paper, *The Argus*, and laid it out on our coffee table amongst the receipt balls and tea rings. I'd go through every job advert with a pen, crossing through any that were too far, didn't offer enough hours, required specialist qualifications or were too vague or obviously dodgy.

I was meant to be doing all the things I used to talk about and I was doing nothing.

Sunday. I was on the bed reading when the Traffic Warden came and stood in the doorway, eating bread straight from the bag.

He spoke with his mouth full. "My mum's invited us for dinner."

I sat up. "Why are you eating bread?"

He shrugged. "Hungry." His hair was damp round the edges with sweat.

"Is it a roast?"

"Of course. It's Sunday."

"So?"

He dropped the bread bag and ran over and tackled me back onto the bed. He lay on top of me so I couldn't move.

When I'd stopped laughing, I said, "You're sweaty," and rubbed my thumb up his forehead and into his hair. "Your hair suits you this length. It's not marine and it's not Stig of the Dump."

He lifted up my T-shirt and spoke to my stomach. "Are you going to come then, Belly?"

"Yeah."

His parents only lived about ten minutes away, so I was surprised when the Traffic Warden started heading for his car.

"Let's walk."

"Nah."

"Why not? Weather's good. We should make the most of it."

"Nah."

He kept going towards his car, so I followed. "One day it'll be too late."

I hadn't meant to sound so ominous.

His mum was waiting for us at the front door. She'd done her hair and I wondered what she made of me, turning up in a T-shirt that was semi-clean at best and old flip-flops. She had a new tablecloth. It was sage green, and she'd put a cream crochet runner down the middle and a vase of flowers in the centre.

It felt very strange to sit on plump cream chairs that all matched. His dad sat at one end of the table and he sat at the other; his mum and I sat in between.

I started with the vegetables, as always. I like to eat a roast in a specific order.

"So how are you?" she asked me.

"I'm fine. Still job-hunting."

"It's hard, isn't it?"

"Yeah. You sort of have to evaluate what you've done and ultimately realise how little it is."

She smiled benignly. "I'm sure you've done lots."

"Not really. Got an interview, though."

"Oh, that's good. What for?"

"Data entry."

"That sounds promising."

"Promising of boredom," the Traffic Warden said.

His mum speared a potato. "Well, we've all got to start somewhere."

Big Nathan

The book was about torture.

The main character caught wasps and fed them into the middle of a trap he'd rigged up from an old town clock, each number representing a different way to die.

The book wouldn't fit in my only smart bag, and I realised on the train that I was going to have to sit with *The Wasp Factory* on my lap during the interview. Or hide it.

As the train eased into the platform I looked at the insects swarming on the cover and imagined being asked what the book was about by some chipper interviewer and saying, deadpan, "Torturing animals."

The woman I had spoken to on the phone earlier that week had told me that the office was only a short walk from the train station – "Just follow the road round until you reach us" – but right outside were a roundabout and four possible roads to follow.

Ip dip, sky blue,
Nanny sitting on the loo,
Singing songs, dropping bombs,
Out goes you.

The last road left didn't really seem that promising, but I followed it and sure enough, halfway up the hill there was a square prefab with a doorbell and three labels, one saying *Weblands* with a dull blue business logo.

"Hello?" The voice was fuzzy but I was fairly sure it was the same woman I had spoken to on the phone.

"Hi, I'm here for the interview."

"Come up to the first floor," she said.

The door buzzed and there was a click as the catch released.

The stairwell seemed very dark after being outside, and it smelt dry, like plaster. When I opened the door marked *Weblands* with the same generic business logo, I found myself in a strange L shape created by a couple of brown screens, strategically placed so I couldn't see how big or small the office was.

The voice on the intercom belonged to a short lady who wore a long skirt and cork wedges, which struck me as a strange choice for someone who looked almost sixty. I smiled and held *The Wasp Factory* behind my back. "You're... Mary."

"Yes, that's me. If you'd like to take a seat, our managing director will be with you shortly." She clasped her hands together and tipped her head on one side, like a saint in a stained-glass window. "Would you like a drink of anything?"

Anything. "Um... water?"

"That's fine, fine. Take a seat." She motioned to a line of three low chairs, made of the same brown fabric as the screens that sectioned me off from the office.

The weather was hot and my clothes were stifling and prickly, like electricity on my skin. My previous job had come with a uniform that consisted of a polo shirt and a pair of men's trousers, so I wasn't used to the tightness of cotton shirts in my armpits.

Mary brought me the water in a glass with a base as heavy as a paperweight and sides so thin that I didn't want to hold it too tightly in case the thing shattered in my fingers.

I went over all the lies I had in my head, about why I wanted this job, what skills I had, where I saw myself in five years' time.

After fifteen minutes, Mary poked her head round one of the screens. "Sorry to have to ask you this, but we need you to sit a typing test."

"Okay, that's fine."

I followed her into the office, where about twenty people sat at an array of desks, some on the phone and some typing, and a woman stood at the printer, hand on hip. I sat down at the computer Mary had gestured towards.

It was opposite a guy who looked about my age, wearing a white shirt with a thin blue grid on it, like graph paper. He didn't look up. I set the book face-down on the desk beside me.

The test was ancient and difficult, and I knew that I was scoring badly even while I was doing it, despite the fact that I was a good typist.

When I was done I sat back and Mary came and clicked a few buttons and noted my score on a Post-it note.

Then I sat back down on the brown chair and waited for a further ten minutes with nothing to stare at but the brown screen before a clean, tall man approached me.

I stood up holding the book behind my back, smiled and shook his hand.

"I'm Nathan?" His voice was slightly high for a man his age and he pronounced it like a question.

I followed him back downstairs, through the door of another office, into a room made of glass and blinds and a huge table of laminated wood.

While he was examining my CV I slipped *The Wasp Factory* under my left thigh and realised that my shoes had rubbed streaks of polish onto my stockings.

He said, "This won't be a formal interview."

I felt pretty formal, but I folded my hands on my lap and smiled and said, "Okay."

"We like to keep things informal here."

I wasn't sure what response he might expect to that, so I nodded without a word.

"So. You graduated... two months ago."

"Yes."

"What did you think of university?"

I tried to think what kind of answer he would like and decided that if I sounded like I was a poor girl who'd worked hard that might be something good.

I weaved my fingers together and put them round my knee. "Well, I was lucky to go," I said. "I learnt a lot. I came across books and ideas that I would never have otherwise."

"Anything else?"

I rolled my thumbs around each other. "Um, I don't know. I guess I learnt what it is that I really want to do in life."

"What is that?"

I felt that I had fallen straight into the first trap. I should've sensed the danger.

"Well, I'd like to work in publishing. Or in a library. Something creative. Something with books would be good."

He smiled.

I smiled back.

An interviewer makes up their mind about you in the first sixty seconds, so I knew the battle was already lost or won.

"You worked in McDonald's while you were at university."

"Yes."

"What did you think of it?"

I had to find some way of side-stepping saying I had hated it. "Well, even though I don't agree with the ethics of their business, I did learn a lot while I was there."

"You became a manager."

"After a year, yes."

"What was that like?"

"It was okay. Not always easy. I worked hard for the money. I had to train people, and I also dealt with some cash and safe duties, and with customer complaints. I enjoyed it in some ways. Working for a big corporation is… an interesting experience."

"Well, we're a fairly small office."

"I want to work somewhere that's different to what I've done before."

That wasn't a lie, but it wasn't the whole truth. I had applied for a data entry position principally because it didn't seem to require any contact with the general public. I had this dreamy idea of a solitary desk by the window, the sun making warm rectangles on my papers, tea on tap and a pot plant with dark green leaves.

Perhaps I could be happy here.

Perhaps I could spend my days unfulfilled but also undisturbed and slowly, slowly, fade into anonymity.

"Okay, well, the job does involve some telephone work. About one per cent."

"Okay." The dream faded slightly, but I could cope with one per cent.

"I mean, you'll very much be a part of the office."

I thought he might just be saying that to make me feel better, so I said, "That sounds good."

He narrowed his eyes at me and for a moment I wondered what he was thinking. Then he glanced back at my CV, then at me again, and a silence hung in the room, floating with the summer dust.

*

When the Traffic Warden got in from work he went straight to the fridge, pulled out a block of cheese and bit right into it. "How did it go?"

I was reading on the sofa and lowered the book but didn't sit up. "I really wish you wouldn't do that." It was one of his many annoying habits, like putting empty bottles back in the fridge and leaving the bread bag open.

"I really wish you wouldn't speak." He paused and craned his neck to watch something out of the kitchen window, which overlooked the car parking area for all the flats in our block.

"It was all right, anyway. I think," I said. "I don't know. It was a strange one. Hard to predict."

He was still looking out the kitchen window.

"Something interesting going on?"

He spoke through another mouthful of cheese. "Mini Man's welding."

Mini Man lived in Flat 4 with his moody girlfriend and their daughter Jessica, a toddler who was always crying. The only times I saw him were when he went out front to have a fag, or when he was in the courtyard tinkering about with his Mini. It looked like he'd made the whole thing from scrap parts as it was about two feet shorter than a normal Mini and rust-coloured, apart from the black roof, which he could just take off whenever he felt like it.

"Fascinating," I said.

"He's got all the gear and everything. I wonder where he learnt to do all that stuff."

"Why don't you ask him?"

The Traffic Warden didn't respond.

"How was work, anyway?"

"All right."

"How many tickets did you give out?"

"Eight."

That night as we were getting into bed, he pulled back the cover and seemed to scrutinise the pillows.

I leaned over. "That's dribble, I think."

"I know." He picked the pillows up and banged them together like cymbals. "I've seen loads of spiders lately, I don't want them crawling on me in the night. Did you know that you swallow eight spiders—"

"—every year. You don't, though. It's an urban myth." I sighed. "It was made up by this woman who made up a load of similar facts and put them on a website, just to see if people would believe them. And what d'you know? They did." I leaned back on the pillows. "I mean, the spider's effectively committing suicide. Why would a spider do that?"

He got in bed, lifting the duvet clean off me.

"Oi, that was warm, don't let all the cold in." I settled my head on his shoulder. "And don't steal it, like you did last night."

"Me? It was me who didn't get any."

"What absolute bollocks. I woke up *twice* with cold feet." I kissed him and felt his hand in my hair.

"You're so dramatic."

I put my leg over his. "And *you* are the Duvet Thief. It's what you are in your very core and you know it." I kissed him again. "And you know that I know it."

And he kissed me back, and climbed on top of me, practically ripping my T-shirt off.

I was surprised when the phone woke me the next morning, and it was Nathan telling me I had the job.

Mel

"So, this is an agreement." A tanned woman called Mel was showing me how to enter agreements into the database. "These are all the details you need to enter. So you've got Name…"

She typed the name.

"Tab along, and then the date of birth."

She typed the date of birth.

"Tab along and the address."

She typed the address.

"Tab along and the start date."

And on.

And on.

I nodded and nodded, until I thought I'd be sick.

I was glad that the work was monotonous, but the atmosphere in the office was slightly awkward, a party of strangers thrown together when there was nothing to talk about, nothing to say.

My dream of a sunlit desk had dissolved; there was nothing but blind windows and a busy road humming behind them.

Weblands officially broke for lunch at one, Mel said, but she and I were to have ours at twelve because they wanted someone to answer the phone over lunch and that someone was her. Soon to be me.

We both got our neat boxes of sandwiches from the fridge and sat opposite each other. There was no canteen or anything, so we just sat at our desks while everyone carried on pecking away at their keyboards.

"What you got?" I asked her.

"Cheese," she said. She held the sandwich with both hands, as if it was going to break apart.

I asked her why she was leaving.

"Just time to move on," she said.

I had hoped for a genuine answer, but she gave me the diplomatic one. I suppose I would have done the same, if I was talking to someone who was about to start the job that I was leaving.

"Oh, right. How long have you worked here?"

"Too long." She finished her sandwich, wiped her fingers on a sheet of kitchen roll dotted with little clouds.

She fiddled with the frill along the shoulder strap of her yellow top. Like all the other women, she was dressed more casually than me.

I had decided it was better to be too formal than not formal enough, and the week before I had bought five white, collared shirts from Matalan. They looked like school shirts, lined up in my wardrobe with a crease down each sleeve.

"Are they quite lax about dress code here?"

"Yeah, they are now, but they weren't always." She glanced over the office at Nathan's desk, and even though it was empty as he'd gone off somewhere, she lowered her voice slightly. "When I first started, women weren't allowed to wear trousers."

"You're kidding."

"No. That was when Nathan's dad was still running the place. I didn't like it, so one day I wore this three-quarter-length trouser suit. It was smart, you know, grey. Roy called me in for a private word."

"Seriously?"

"Yeah. He never let me wear them. But then Nathan took over, and he's a lot more laidback when it comes to that sort of thing."

"That's so old-fashioned."

"I know. It's not like anyone ever comes up here."

On the way home, I walked along the train platform until I reached the furthest bench still under shelter. I felt people's eyes on me, and was aware that I was a new face amongst them.

A man paced between me and the tracks, his shoes making soft scuffing sounds on the dusty concrete of the platform. He had a helmet hanging off his rucksack but no bike, and I thought how funny it was that everyone assumed he had a bike chained up at the other end of the station when maybe he didn't even own a bike, but just carried the helmet because he was paranoid about loose masonry or the sky falling.

He could be insane and no one would know.

When I got back to the flat, the Traffic Warden was standing in the doorway in socks, his uniform shirt untucked.

I stood on tiptoe and kissed him, and moved past.

"How was it?"

"Fine."

The truth was, it didn't much matter; it was the only place that had even given me an interview. I went into the front room and saw that the Xbox was on, paused on a battle scene.

"Have you thrown out the box for that yet?" I asked.

"No, and I'm not going to, either."

Ever since I'd known him, he'd kept the box of any electrical appliance he bought, so we had quite a collection growing on top of the wardrobe. It seemed bizarre to me, as if he thought all our things were just borrowed, and one day he was going to have to slot everything back into its place and we would start our lives for real.

He un-paused the game. "Was it really fine?"

I slipped off my shoes and sprawled on the sofa. "Well, I'm never going to love it."

"I don't know why you don't just become a traffic warden, like me."

The thought of our matching fluorescent jackets hanging off the living-room door and two sets of epaulettes on the table made me queasy. "Are you mental?"

"It's such easy money. Once you can handle people having a pop at you all day long, it's a piece of cake."

"Not in a gazillion fucking years."

He shook his head. "I don't get you at all."

Mary

On my second day, I must've looked pale because when Mary swished past my desk to get some envelopes from up the back, she asked me if I was okay.

"Toothache," I said, touching my cheek. It felt warm.

"Didn't look after them when you were a student?" she asked. I wondered how she knew I had been a student, as I hadn't really said anything about myself to anyone.

"It's not that. I think my wisdom teeth are coming through."

"You'll have to pay now, you know." There was a strange tone to her voice that I knew wasn't as friendly as it was supposed to appear.

"Yes," I said. "I suppose I will."

On the train platform that evening I went to the same bench and watched people milling about to see which ones I recognised from the day before. An observation test, and I had plenty of time to look as there were two fast trains to Brighton, the 17.10 and the 17.16, before my train, the 17.24.

Helmet Man was there again, pacing on the dusty ground.

Just before the 17.16 a woman with cropped hair and two canvas bags sat beside me on the bench, put her bags down and took out a book, all in one fluid motion. She opened the book and started reading straight away, as if she'd never been interrupted from it.

The 17.16 pulled in and she didn't get on it, so I knew she needed a stop before Brighton and would get on the 17.24 with me. I wondered which station was hers.

It's always fascinated me that everyone you see outside your house has a different destination in mind.

My third day was Mel's last; she was part-time, so her working week was over.

At 11.26 she went to the toilet and Mary rushed over to my desk on her wedges with a bright yellow folder. "Quick, sign this, it's Mel's leaving card."

"Oh, right, thanks." I added my name to the other signatures, closed the folder and handed it back.

"You'll miss her, won't you?" Mary said, her head on one side.

"Yeah."

"Well, don't worry. I'm sure you'll be fine."

At about four, everyone gathered round Mel's desk and I watched as Nathan presented her with a mock-pewter statue of a dancer in a graceful pose.

It was impossible to tell from her reaction whether she liked it or not.

At five she checked through her drawers, picked up her bag and got up to go. "Well, this is all yours now."

"Thanks," I said. "And good luck in your new job." I ran my eyes over her desk, now mine. The only personal effects were a plastic pig sitting on the monitor and a Robbie Williams mouse mat.

"Don't you want the pig?" I held it out to her and realised that it wasn't plastic but a spongy corporate stress toy.

"That belonged to the girl who was here before me, and when she went away she said I should look after it. So I'll pass that on to you."

"What about Robbie?" I wanted her to take the mouse mat because I hated him with a passion, but she shook her head.

"Oh, he isn't mine, he just lives here." She smiled. "Actually, I can't stand him."

On the train home, I started to feel almost faint with toothache. I watched Reading Woman get on the train with me, and although this time I looked out at every station, I didn't see her get off.

The Traffic Warden was standing in the flat's doorway, barefoot and still in his uniform, eating slices of salami from a packet. He must have seen me coming up the road.

"Hello," I said. The corridor echoed so badly that my voice boomed out. I kissed him while still holding my face and went straight to the cupboard where we kept mugs and medicine.

He followed me, still chewing. "Just book an appointment, will you?"

"I don't have a dentist down here." I didn't have anything down here.

"My mum can recommend one."

"I hate the dentist."

"Who doesn't? When was the last time you went?"

"About three years ago."

"Well, it's not a surprise you've got toothache then, is it?"

"Thank you, doctor."

"It'll only get worse."

"Yes, thank you."

"How was work, anyway?" he asked. I could see the salami churning round his mouth, like a pink shirt in the wash.

"Well…" I took a pair of Anadin and sipped some water. "I'm not going to stop buying *The Argus*."

I looked out the kitchen window to the courtyard below, as a nurse hurried across the damp concrete to where her car was parked.

As far as I could work out, the nurses came for the old woman in the downstairs flat. While I was unemployed I had seen them coming every morning and every evening, but they varied so much I could tell they all came from a bank of casual workers that was most likely council-run.

Strangely, though, they all behaved in a very similar fashion, as if one had trained the others to be precisely like her. They always parked between two spaces, spent about half an hour in the old woman's flat – if not less – and went. They all wore crisp white tunics and plain black trousers, had fluffy animals hanging off their keys, and leapt in their cars and drove off.

The old woman must have been housebound to get twice-daily visits, but the weird thing was I never saw her, or any of the nurses, take a rubbish bag to the bin shed, and they never brought her shopping. I never saw any visitors.

I couldn't fathom it.

"That Mercedes is there again." The Traffic Warden was looking over my shoulder.

"What Mercedes?" My jaw still felt hot but I could feel the pain receding slightly.

"There's only one."

It was parked right next to where the nurse had been. "So?"

"So she parks her posh car here and goes into town because she's too cheap to spend sixty pee on a fucking ticket."

"Perhaps that's how she can afford a Mercedes."

"Are we going shopping, then?"

"I guess so."

After two months of living with the Traffic Warden it was obvious that our trips round the supermarket had changed from when we'd been students.

We were not stoned and in pyjamas, there to pick up ready-made potato wedges and muffins and chocolate milk and fags and then speed back to the warmth of my messy bedroom. Suddenly we were a Young Couple who had a small trolley together instead of a basket each and argued over salt content and what bread to get.

I wrenched a trolley from the line and pushed it through the huge open doorway.

"Hey, let's play Wife Beater." It was an old game.

He tilted his head to look at the papers on the stand. "No."

"Oh, go on."

He grabbed my elbow and bellowed, his teeth close to my face. "Will-you-fucking-shut-up-you-stupid-bitch?"

I bowed my head and just caught the expression on a woman's face before she went off to Fruit 'n' Veg. I knew that we would be destined to see her again, in the frozen aisle, or gazing at cheese, and she would stare at us and pity me and then look away.

We got to teabags, stacked on the shelves like children's wooden blocks. I held his arm, leaning my head against it.

He looked over the boxes. "Normal or…"

"Normal," I said. "Come on, I don't want to spend my whole evening in here."

He picked up a box of green tea and started reading the back, God knows what for. "I think I'm going to try these."

"They all taste like pond water."

"Don't be stupid."

"You're stupid. You won't drink them." I said it because I knew that even if it turned out he didn't like them, he'd drink them to spite me.

He didn't move.

"Let's go." I pulled on his sleeve. "They're tea bags, for God's sake. It's not like you're deciding what to do with the rest of your life."

In Crisps 'n' Nuts, the Traffic Warden picked me up and swung me over his shoulder fireman-style, like he used to. I laughed until I saw a man standing by a trolley, his wife next to him bending to look at a label.

The man looked so washed-out and pathetic, like an old cloth, and I thought, *One day we won't laugh any more and we'll be just like you.*

And then I couldn't enjoy the moment any more and I flopped into dead weight, so the Traffic Warden brought me down, our bellies scraping together.

He gave me a kiss on the lips, but I was still aware of the man watching us.

"What's up?" the Traffic Warden asked.

I looked away. "Nothing."

*

Friday night. I was sitting on the edge of the bath, brushing my teeth.

The Traffic Warden came and stood in the doorway. "Get out."

"I'm doing my teeth."

"I need a piss."

"So? I'm not stopping you."

"You know I don't like it when there are other people in the room."

"I was here first."

He went to pick me up, so I took my brush out, tipped my head back, and made ready to blow froth in his face.

"You wouldn't dare."

I spoke through foam. "Oh, wouldn't I?"

"Come on, just go."

I blew out, so his glasses got covered in white specks.

"Right!" He got me by the arms but I blew again, spitting more froth. Neither of us could fight for laughing, and I had to lean over and dribble the rest in the sink.

"You really are disgusting," he said.

"You love me, though."

"You're a bint. Now get out."

Kim

For seven and a half hours of each day I sat opposite an empty desk, and for the other half-hour it was occupied by Kim.

Normally, she sat with Mary, Ian and the guy who wore shirts checked like graph paper – who was also called Nathan – but each afternoon she came over for half an hour to use that computer.

While Mel had been there Kim had completely ignored me, but now when she came over she smiled as she sat down.

"Hello," I said.

She was pregnant and placed her hands across her bump.

"Congratulations, by the way," I said.

She wore her hair in a ponytail that was so loose it might just as well have been left down. "Oh, thanks."

"It must feel amazing to be pregnant."

"Oh, yeah, it does – I get loads of attention."

I laughed, but she didn't, and just continued to stare at me, rubbing the bump.

"What are you doing?" I asked.

"Submission." She didn't elaborate.

Later, I saw her whispering to the younger Nathan, and I caught her eyes flicking in my direction.

Julia

"You aren't Mel."

"No, I'm not."

After a fortnight of picking up the phone at Weblands, I was well used to this. Some days I felt as if I was explaining to people that the flat, barely-awake voice they heard was the replacement of their very own guardian angel.

"I'm her replacement."

"Oh, I see. And what's your name?"

This *was* unusual. As if to deny my very existence, all other people who rang just went on to tell me who they were calling to speak to, and I would take a name and company and put them through or ask them if they'd like to hold. I understood the pain of the automated service, from the robot's perspective.

I told the caller my name.

"Well, this is Julia." She sounded a bit like an old-fashioned nanny; she had a steady confidence that gained my instant respect and compliance, and I started to feel as if she had done me a massive favour that I would never repay.

"Oh, right. Who are you wanting to speak to?"

"Ian, if I may."

"Okay. Bear with me." I dialled Ian's extension as quickly as I could. I had everyone's numbers on a sheet tacked to my in-tray, but I'd memorised them by this point.

Ian almost always asked me to tell people he was on the other line or in a meeting, but as soon as I told him it was Julia he cleared his throat and said, "Go ahead."

Next time she rang was about a week later. I was in the middle of sorting a pile of transmittal forms into alphabetical order when I picked up and said my usual slogan in my usual tone. "Good morning, you're through to reception, how can I help?"

"Hello. How are you?"

I recognised the voice instantly. "Oh. I'm fine, thanks. And you?"

"Yes, thank you, not bad. Hoping the good weather holds out."

"Me too. Do you want Ian?"

"No, it's Nathan I rang for this time. Big Nathan, not Young Nathan. Is he there?"

I looked over my shoulder. He was sitting in his usual position behind his enormous semi-circular desk, calmly typing into his silver laptop. He always looked too perfect and straight and clean, like something out of a health and safety video.

"He is," I said to Julia. "Bear with me."

"Thank you," she said, her voice oozing like honey. "You're ever so kind."

Ruth

In those weeks after Mel left, I felt myself setting a strict routine, ruled by the clock on my reception phone. I started work at the exact stroke of 9.00. I stopped at exactly 12.00, started again at exactly 13.00, and stopped at 17.00.

I did absolutely no more, and no less, than what was asked of me.

My main job was to enter the agreements into the database, file the transmittal forms that came with them, send some of the post out, and pick up the reception phone.

I was too much of an anomaly to have my own island, so I sat on the edge of customer services, next to Ruth.

She wasn't fat but she was big-built, and sat on her chair like a great bird of paradise. She wore a headset so she could type and talk at the same time, and sometimes, when I felt exceptionally bored, I pretended I was her co-pilot.

She was there when I arrived in the morning.

She was there when I left in the evening.

She didn't stop for lunch.

I spoke to her only to ask her work-related questions about the agreements.

There was evidence of Secret Santas from years past on her desk: a fluffy reindeer clung to the back of her post tray, and she had a mug that said *Sensible Shoes* in letters constructed from pink dots above a picture of a pink stiletto. It had clearly been picked in desperation by someone who didn't know her very well, and I admired her for displaying an object so at odds with her personality.

One day, I got up at 17.00 and said, "Goodbye, everyone," to all of the customer services.

No one even looked up.

*

I was smoking by the big window in our living room, which was west-facing and gave the best view of the sunset. The Traffic Warden had realised this before I'd moved in, and set up a deckchair there which had fast become one of my favourite places, especially since our sofa was about as comfortable as sitting in a cardboard box.

I could see Mini Man and his girlfriend outside, smoking on the wall together. God, she looked moody.

I opened the window and heard a train rumble out of the station, where they went to London in forty minutes and Brighton in twenty. I didn't feel particularly close to anything, though perhaps I should have.

I had waited for more trains in the last month than I'd thought I would in my whole life, and I didn't feel like I was going anywhere.

"We might as well live in the middle of fucking nowhere," I said.

Absorbed in Ceefax, the Traffic Warden said nothing.

*

On my fourth Monday, I woke up having barely slept, and I sat on the toilet with heaviness in my bones, watching a spider climb into a hole in the side of the bath. It'd made a sort of web hammock between the hole and the wall, but I didn't think it would catch many flies as it was flecked with white paint.

When I got out of the shower I opened the window. The air was cold and the sky was grey and I felt deeply sick, like when the summer holidays were over and I had to go back to school. I leaned over the toilet to puke but nothing came out.

The Traffic Warden was on a late, which meant that he started at nine, and as his base was in the council building down the road from my office, he gave me a lift to work.

He kept banging the steering wheel as he drove, ranting about mums and their four-by-fours.

I had heard it all before and looked out the window at the world passing. I thought that if the next twenty-four years of my life were anything like the last I would kill myself.

Eventually he pulled into the road by my office and waited for me to get out.

I looked at his dashboard, still encrusted with the chocolate milk drips from our student days, and thought about the week ahead.

To my own surprise I started to cry, and the tears felt big and hot on my face. Perhaps the Traffic Warden had seen it coming because he held me against him, my snot disappearing into his soft black uniform jumper.

"Oh, you delicate flower." He fiddled with my hair, running his fingers over the top of my head, and touched my ears, my wet cheeks, my red nose. "I forget, sometimes, what a delicate flower you are."

I wanted to say that I wasn't a delicate flower at all, but I didn't say anything. I just waited for the feeling to dissipate. All the hugs

34

in the world wouldn't save me.

"Do you want me to take you home?"

"No."

"I don't mind."

"Please, it's fine really. I'm sorry, I'm being an idiot."

"Go on, call in sick."

I looked at the clock on his car radio. It was 9.05. I wiped my face, and kissed him squarely on his lips, holding his face in my hands. "See you tonight." And before I could stop myself, I got up and out of the car.

Weblands shared its building with two other companies and sat between them on the first floor, like limbo.

I didn't want anyone to see me, so I washed my face in the downstairs toilet of the building. The water was freezing and turned my fingers white. When I looked in the mirror after I had dried off, my eyes were red. It was clear that it wouldn't make any difference how much I washed.

I went up and collapsed into my seat. The time on my phone said 9.15. That would come out of my lunch. I bent down beneath my desk to turn my computer on.

"We thought you weren't coming in," Ruth said.

"Sorry. Argument with boyfriend."

Whenever I referred to the Traffic Warden as my boyfriend, I almost felt that I was talking about someone else. Boyfriend, lover, partner. Nothing really fit. There had always been something slightly indescribable about him.

My phone started ringing.

"Well." Ruth's voice was kind, quieter than normal. "Don't worry about your phone for five minutes. Get yourself sorted first. Have a cup of tea or something."

35

Her kindness only served to depress me more as I realised it was the first time she had said something to me that wasn't strictly work-related, when I'd been sitting less than four feet away from her every day for three weeks.

All day I entered agreements. I watched my own fingers on the keyboard and occasionally glanced out of the window at the dark clouds rolling across.

At 12.15, I went to lunch and Mary took the phone as she always did. I got my sandwiches from the fridge and ate them at my desk while doing Google image searches for storms. The best ones were satellite photos of tropical cyclones that showed swirls of cloud with huge, deep eyes in the centre.

I tried to imagine what it would be like to stand in that eye, right in the middle of all that power but where the storm is calmest.

When I got home, I did the washing-up while I waited for the Traffic Warden. At ten past six when he got in, he put down his bag and regarded me with gentle eyes. "Were you very late this morning?"

We hugged, me on tiptoes, and I could feel the sharpness of his bristly chin on my forehead. "No, not too bad."

"What did you tell them?"

"I said we had an argument."

"You need to get out of there."

"I know." And I squeezed him as if trying to pop him, until he laughed.

I wondered if this would still work in twenty years, or if he would grow bored of it.

We rocked together in the kitchen, almost like dancing. All I could hear was the fridge humming.

He said, "That Mercedes is there again."

After dinner, I Googled "wisdom teeth" and read stories of people having their jaws broken, waking up woozy and not knowing where they were.

I said nothing to the Traffic Warden, but took two Anadin and laid out *The Argus* on our coffee table.

After going through my usual ritual, I was left with four jobs. Three of them I had already done in the past and didn't want to do again.

I started working on a CV. Qualifications. Dates. Grades.

After a few hours the Traffic Warden got up and went to the bathroom and when he came back he was brushing his teeth. "What you doing?" He spoke through his toothbrush, and I could see flecks of white coming off his lips.

"CV."

"You coming to bed?"

Work. Duties. References. "Okay."

*

I was filing barefoot when Mary brushed past me on her way to the envelope cupboard at the back. "Be careful with your bare feet, won't you?" she said. "There may be stray staples."

The thought had occurred to me earlier, but I'd dismissed it.

"I'll be all right." I carried on filing, but did look at my feet as if to check they were still there, and that's when I noticed that the little toenail on my right foot had turned a deep purple.

The nails on my little toes were very small, and I wondered how small something had to be before it became completely insignificant.

When she came back past she said words that I'd come to dread: "Just to let you know, we need more C5 envelopes."

It was another of my jobs to order all the stationery for the office. Mostly this consisted of reams upon reams of paper for customer service printouts, and a mind-boggling array of envelopes. There were three different sizes: DL, C5, and C4. Some had windows and some didn't; some had to be gummed for the machine and others self-seal; some were over-printed with our address on the back. I couldn't fathom any sort of system to it, and to make matters worse I had to renegotiate a price each time. I just knew that no matter what I asked Mary, or how long I spent poring over the catalogue, I would get the wrong ones.

But I humoured her.

"Window or non?"

"I think window. I'm not sure."

The phone rang at exactly 17.00. This had never happened before, so I wasn't sure what rule applied. Had it been 17.01, I would certainly have left it.

I reasoned that I could tell them our offices had just closed, and that the person they wanted – whoever it was – had gone home. Might take me over to 17.01 or even 17.02, but I couldn't leave it, not with Ruth sitting right next to me mid-email.

I picked it up, and said my line like a mantra.

"Do you want my reference?" she asked me.

I knew instantly that I couldn't help her, as the customer service phones were already off. "Sure."

"Four, one, eight…"

"Okay, well, I'm afraid you've come through to the wrong office, actually. I need to give you the number for the other." I wasn't lying. I didn't know what the other office did; I only knew it was them she needed because she'd quoted a reference number that started with a four. "Have you got a pen and paper handy?"

"Yeah."

"Okay, it's oh-eight-four-five…"

"Hang on, it's not working."

"You'll have to etch it into the paper," I told her, a smile in my voice. I had been in her position. I had written numbers in crayon and barely-there brown felt tip up the side of a takeaway menu or newspaper. "Strange, isn't it? Why do you put a pen back where it was, even though you know it doesn't work?"

The woman hung up.

When I got home, I told the Traffic Warden about my toenail.

He was bent double on the sofa, leaning into his laptop, which he'd set up on the coffee table. He had his thumb resting on the top of his wide-open mouth and looked as if he was staring into a portal to a parallel universe, although I knew that he was browsing articles on BBC Sport.

"It might fall off," I said.

He ignored me.

"My head fell off earlier, but I sewed it back on."

He took his thumb out of his mouth and sat up. "Do you want to join a gym?"

I couldn't think of anything I'd rather do less. "No."

"Why not?"

"Because I can't think of anything I'd rather do less."

"You could gouge your own eyes out."

I kicked my shoes off, the thick rubber soles jarring on the carpet. I looked at my nail, still purple, still there. "I'd prefer it."

A week later, we went to the gym.

I wasn't a sport person, and had to rifle through my bottom

drawer to find any clothes that might be even slightly appropriate. I found some old jogging bottoms that were two inches too short, and my only clean T-shirt was a sickly shade of green.

"I feel like I've just rifled through the lost property box."

"Who cares what you look like?" He had old shorts and trainers on and despite never making any effort with his clothes, he still looked better than me.

"No one, I guess." I wiped a clump of hair behind my ear.

"Are you ready?"

I hugged him, partly so he wouldn't be able to see me. "No."

We had an induction where a bald guy in a pale blue gym T-shirt explained things to me like, "This is a bike," and, "This is the screen," and, tapping through the options on a keypad, "There are programs you can use," but he said nothing about what the different programs were, or what any of the numbers meant.

I looked at the Traffic Warden to pull a face, but he was just nodding through it all.

Then we were left in the near-deserted gym to have our first session.

I was reluctant to even get on anything, worried it would fall over or I would use it wrong. The bikes looked easy, so I got on one of them. I don't know what I was expecting, but after getting over the initial sensation of being on a bike that didn't go anywhere, I found I had very little to look at or think about while I was doing it.

For a while I watched the calorie counter, but that depressed me for a number of reasons, so I gave up on that and looked around at the only other people in there. A girl in pink jogging shorts was reading a magazine while on the stair machine. She looked very tanned. She looked like she really loved herself. A guy in a sweaty red T-shirt was doing weights in the aisle and blowing his cheeks out whenever he lunged forward, and I watched the sweat patches bloom on his T-shirt, fading into existence like Rorschach blots. One on his back looked like an upside-down bird, screaming towards earth.

As soon as I started to feel like a hamster in a wheel or a lab rat in mindless regular motion, I knew I wasn't going to be able to stand it twice a week, not for all the promises of firm thighs in the world.

"What did you think?" the Traffic Warden asked when we came out. His face was sweaty and red and he was wiping himself over with a towel.

I thought of my little toenail.

"It was okay," I said.

*

Kim came over one day to do submission.

"What you up to tonight?" she asked.

"Nothing much," I said. "You?" Over the course of a few weeks, I had systematically discovered that we disagreed on everything, but pathetically I looked forward to her coming over. At least she spoke to me.

"Me and Craigy have to go and look at four-by-fours."

I started laughing, but she didn't follow me. "What, those massive cars?"

"Yeah. We'll need one for when Tinkerbell's born." She caught the expression on my face, subtle though it must have been. "I'm not really going to name it Tinkerbell. It's just what I call it now." She rubbed her bump.

"Oh, right." Strange for a nearly new mother to refer to her baby as *it*.

"Yeah, so I have to trade in my lovely Beetle." She ran a nail down her cheek to imply an empty tear track and started speaking in the voice of a six-year-old. "I don't want to get rid of her."

"Why are you doing it, then?" I asked.

Her eyes narrowed slightly. "You have to fit a lot of stuff in with a baby, you know."

There didn't seem much point in arguing about it. "Right."

The next desk along from the one Kim used for submission was Kyle's.

Kyle was about twenty, and must have spent at least half an hour each morning carving his beard – it was always the same sharp line, framing his jaw as if it had been drawn on – and yet he never ironed his shirt, or knotted his tie properly.

He worked in customer services, taking inbound calls. It was pitifully ironic that he would pick up the phone and say, "Good morning, help line," because firstly, he never really helped anyone, and secondly, if anyone needed help, it was him.

"So have you been to university?" he asked me.

"Yeah." I opened my drawer and took out an apple, aware of Kim's eyes on me.

"Was it good?" Kyle asked.

I took a bite of the apple and thought of our old house with its rotten kitchen, the mould in the sink, the furniture falling apart, the pub carpet in my bedroom, those long days in the library struggling to write essays on subjects about which I knew nothing. "Yeah. It was great. Are you going?"

"Well, I wanted to," he said. "But it seems like a waste of money."

"It's not."

"I really respect what Kelly's doing," Kim said.

Kelly was sixteen and wore a lot of eyeliner, and sat on the other side of Ruth. She looked up from her computer at the sound of her name but she didn't say anything.

Kim went on. "You know, she's left school and she's getting on with work."

I knew exactly where this was going.

The last time I had seen my mum, she asked me what the point of university had been, now it was all over. We were in the car and I opened my window a few inches to feel the air rushing in my face.

I said, "I learnt stuff."

She said, "Yeah, like what?"

And I told her about the difference between the written world and the unwritten world, how it wasn't just the case that language reflected the world but that it shaped it too, how language defined our lives and thoughts more than we really thought.

She stared through the windscreen for a beat and then said, "Well, you've just told me that in three minutes. What about the rest of the time?"

"Well, there's obviously other stuff." For a minute I thought about going into it, but I knew it was pointless.

"I mean, look at Young Nathan," Kim was going on. "He left university like you, spent all that money on it so now he's in loads of debt, and he still can't get the job he wants because he doesn't have office experience."

"Doesn't make it a waste of time."

"When Kelly's your age, she's going to be earning much more money than you are." Kim smiled, and for an instant, I hated her.

"It's not just about money, though, is it?"

Kelly spoke up. "What is it about?"

"Ideas." And as I said it, I became aware that I hadn't had many of those lately.

When Kim had finished submission and was gone, I went over to the stationery cupboard, and took three brand new biros out of the box. First, I put them in my drawer and went back to entering a few agreements. Then, when I was certain that no one was looking, I slipped them into my bag, one by one.

Mary came over with an envelope in her hand. "These C5 envelopes are the wrong ones."

"Oh."

"We need window, not non-window. Now we've effectively got two boxes of useless envelopes."

"Sorry, I thought you wanted non-window. I'll order some others today. Sorry about that."

Mary smiled a little. "It's fine," she said. "We all make mistakes."

When I left the office that evening I realised that it had started to get dark early and already seemed like night.

The 17.10 and the 17.16 were both delayed, so there was no room at my usual bench, and it was raining, so everyone on the platform had gathered under the corrugated iron roof with their phones and bags and dripping umbrellas.

I wanted to be far away from all of them, so I wandered the full length of the platform, past Reading Woman and Helmet Man, until I was out of the shelter and could feel the rain on my face.

I heard a loud splashing over my music, and took my earphones out so I could listen to it. The sound was coming from the opposite platform, where the rain was falling off the edge of the roof in a long, arcing rivulet to the concrete like a huge hose. I loved the sound of it, and it was so weird to hear it there in the station.

I breathed in and heard the electric pylons buzzing in the high, wet air.

I felt a wind creeping low along the ground, sweeping round my ankles and making the puddles shiver, and I imagined it gaining speed and pulling things along with it. I imagined the pylons crashing down and the roof of the opposite platform splintering into bits, wires twanging like broken guitar strings and cracking and fizzing and snapping in the rain.

It was properly dark by the time my train came, screeching along the tracks with big sparks flying from the wheels. I looked at the other commuters and they all seemed to be looking at their phones, their watches, the train information.

It was a firework display, just for me, as if I was the only one who could see it.

In the flats two guys were hauling an old bedstead up the stairs outside our door. One of them had a paint-flecked sweatshirt, and the other a grey hoodie.

"Hello." The one in the hoodie. He was about forty, with wiry brown hair and the skin of a smoker.

"All right?" I asked.

He held out a hand and I shook it. His nails were full of dirt. "We're moving in upstairs."

"Grotty day to move. Flat nine?"

"Yeah."

"I live just here."

"Oh, right, below us then."

The Traffic Warden popped out, and I introduced him and then myself.

"I'm Dusty," the one in the hoodie said. "And this is Jason."

The Traffic Warden shook hands too. "Nice to meet you. Do you need any help?"

"Nah, we're all right, ta. Done most of it now anyway."

"Okay, well, we'll let you get on. If you need anything, just knock."

"Yeah, and you."

We went inside and shut the door.

"They seemed all right," I said.

"I don't know," the Traffic Warden muttered darkly. "Look like they might be cunts to me."

Rachel

The week after that, Rachel started at Weblands.

Like me on my first day, she was taken round the office and introduced to everyone.

The whole ritual made me squirm, as I knew from recent experience how awkward it was: the new person was forced to try to say something different to everyone when there are only so many ways to say hello, and all the while they listened to strings of names as if anyone could remember that many faces. For a few days after my introduction, I kept peering round and squinting at people, trying to remember the difference between Matt and Nick until I figured out that Matt always wore black shirts.

I watched Rachel making her way round the office, and when she got to me I swung around in my chair and her middle was at my eye level so I could see straight away that she had a black miniskirt tight across her thighs, with two little slits up the sides. When I looked up at her face to say hi, I saw that her eyes were huge and dark, and her hair was cut into a sharp chocolate bob.

She wouldn't fit into Weblands at all and I liked her instantly.

She'd been taken on as customer service, so she would take inbound calls with Kyle and Kelly. Ruth, head of customer service, was busy that day and so asked me to train her on data input.

I found a chair and hauled it round to my side.

I chose a batch of easy agreements.

The first name was Mrs Julia Glasscock and as I got Rachel to type it in I stifled a smile, but then she turned and I caught her eye and we both giggled.

"Honestly," I said, "if you were going to marry a Mr Glasscock, wouldn't you just keep your own name?"

"I'd dump him."

We talked until lunchtime. She had a law degree and a daughter called Amy. She didn't say anything about a husband.

"How old is she?"

"Eight. Wanna see a picture?"

"Okay."

She ferreted about under the desk for her bag.

"You know, you really don't look old enough to have an eight-year-old," I said.

"I know! Great, isn't it? I'm thirty-five but I swear, most of the time I feel about eighteen."

When my clock hit twelve I was about to get my sandwiches out of the fridge like Pavlov's dog, when she said, "Want a fag?"

I felt relief filter through me.

We left our sandwiches on our desks and when we got outside she spun around with her arms out and said, "Oh my God, do you ever wonder what the fuck you're doing?" She turned and caught the expression on my face and said, "What am I talking about? Of course you do."

Three days later, Ruth started training her in customer service, and after a fortnight she had an inch of filing and was taking phone calls. It meant we couldn't really talk that much, and I was back to solo lunches, but I didn't mind. Rachel still took the empty desk that had been opposite me, so Mark, the IT guy, moved the submission software to the account management island.

This meant that Kim had no reason to come over each day.

Mike

On the day before Halloween, the Traffic Warden suggested we go swimming instead of to the gym.

It had been years since I'd been in a swimming pool and I'd forgotten the sensation of weightless floating that you get in the water.

I stretched my arms out and felt the muscles ache from where they'd been in the same position every day since I'd started sitting at a desk in Weblands. I knew it wouldn't last, but it was good to feel free.

I rolled onto my back and started to swim down the slow lane, watching the strip lights pass on the ceiling like the lines down the middle of the road.

After a few lengths I got tired, and stopped for a rest. I leaned with my shoulders against the tiles at the edge of the pool, kicking my legs out in front of me, and watched the diving pool.

There were about five boys, all skinny and pale as birch branches. One of them, in red trunks, climbed up to the top board and stood with his toes curling over the edge. I felt prickly even watching him, but he just held his arms up and leapt off. I watched him sail through the air and enter the water like a pencil. He'd barely disturbed the surface.

The Traffic Warden swam up beside me. He was really out of breath.

"Take it easy," I said. "You're not training for the Olympics."

"You're certainly not, fatty."

He watched the divers with me for a bit, and I was glad of his company.

"How can they do that?" I asked. "Do you have any idea?"

"What do you mean?"

"I mean, how can they just leap into oblivion like that?"

"I dunno, but I feel like a bit of a paedo watching them."

He pushed off and I watched his splashes the whole length of the pool. As soon as he left the far end to come back, I pushed off myself. I had always loved gliding through the water, streamlined as a fish, or torpedo.

"How did you find that?" the Traffic Warden asked, as we stepped out into the cold air, dripping and stinking of chlorine.

I shrugged. "I don't really get it."

"What do you mean, you don't get it?" He was laughing. "There's nothing to get. It's good exercise. It works all your muscles—"

"Yeah, but what's the goal? I mean, what are we trying to achieve here?"

"Exercise."

"Yeah, I know, but why does it have to be so boring? Just going up and down, up and down. It's better than going to the gym, but it still seems really pointless."

"Why live if we all die anyway?"

"That's not what I mean."

Mike, the old man who lived in the flat below ours, was hunched in the main doorway to the flats when we got back.

I had met him the week after I'd moved in, when the Traffic Warden had dropped a heavy glass bowl on the kitchen floor and he'd come up to see what the noise was. I'd answered the door and introduced myself, and he'd looked right over my shoulder as if I didn't exist and asked for the Traffic Warden, so I wasn't exactly enamoured.

"Hello, Mike," the Traffic Warden said, putting on the voice he used to talk to my parents.

"Oh, hello." He croaked like he'd just been forced to smoke a whole packet of cigarettes, and pretended to be surprised to see us. "You seen my notice about the bins?"

He'd written on the piece of cardboard that comes in packet shirts, in thick black felt pen, and taped it right next to the front door to all the flats. I had seen it, but I turned and read it as if I hadn't.

Please make sure you put bin bag's inside the bins.
We will get rats.
Some of the lose bags have spilt.

"The bins are all full of maggots and flies," I said.

Our bins were still the old type, thick black plastic with *no hot ashes* embossed in the lid, and they were kept in a brick shed in the courtyard. Every time I took the rubbish out I got a faceful of flies that sent me spitting out of the shed.

"I'll write to the council about it if you like," I said, for some reason keen for him to consider us responsible young neighbours. "See if they can sort us out something. We should have wheelie bins really, 'cause they'll never empty them like that. They're disgusting. I'm good at letters."

He didn't smile, but spoke to the Traffic Warden, as if he had said what I'd just said. "We've had those same bins here since 1974."

I carried on. "Well, the dustmen won't pick them up, for good reason, and the rubbish gets compacted at the bottom and rots. I'll write to the council, tell them we need wheelie bins."

Again, he spoke to the Traffic Warden. "Some of us don't *want* wheelie bins."

He said it as if there was an underground sect of people against wheelie bins, and I suddenly felt very sorry for any council workers who had to deal with his complaints.

"I seen a rat," he said to the Traffic Warden. "Last week."

That was the moment I started to hope that a plague of them would come to the bin shed in their droves to feast on our scraps.

Later, I was sitting on the sofa wrapped in a blanket, combing the knots out of my chlorine-smelling hair and watching an old Ruth Rendell murder mystery. I'd loved them when I was a kid and they made me feel about ten again.

All my muscles felt heavy.

"It's raining," the Traffic Warden said. He was smoking by the window.

I opened my mouth to say something, but there was a blue flash and thunder cracked so loudly that I could see why people used to think storms were God being angry.

"Ooh," I said.

"Are you scared?"

"Of the storm? No."

There was another blue flash and a clap of thunder and I counted between them like I always had. "It's close, though," I said. "Are *you* scared?"

We listened to the rain rushing against the window.

"Nah," he said. "I'm not scared of anything."

RTW

I had just reached the bottom of my in-tray for the first time since Mel had left and was wondering what to do with myself, when the buzzer went and someone mumbled into it about opening the door.

As well as doing the data entry and picking up the phone my job included answering that buzzer, although until then it had only been unexciting parcel deliveries and I'd just let the couriers in and signed their clipboards and taken the boxes to their recipients. Nine times out of ten they'd been printer cartridges for Mark the IT guy, or stationery deliveries for me.

This time, though, an old man came in and stood in the doorway. He was tall and had a rugby player's shoulders, though not the suit to go with it, so he looked like a superhero about to burst at the seams.

I was about to get up and ask him who he was, but as soon as Mary saw his head above the brown screen she rushed over and greeted him and offered him a drink.

"No, I'm okay, thank you, just here to see Nathan briefly."

I watched him stride into the office and shake hands with Big Nathan as if he hadn't had to be buzzed up like a delivery of printer ink.

I went over to Mary's desk on the pretence of getting a glass of water from the kitchen and whispered to her, "Who's that?"

She looked almost offended and said, "RTW," as if it was obvious.

I went back to my desk and reached for a new batch of

agreements to type before remembering I'd cleared them all.

It was 14.29.

Rachel was on the phone.

I wasn't used to the feeling of being redundant.

In McDonald's there had always been something to do because when there wasn't they either sent us home to keep labour costs down or made up tasks for us. When I'd first started it had irked me that I couldn't tell the difference between a real and an imaginary task, but after a while I stopped caring what the jobs were and I just did them. I liked feeling useful.

I ran my finger down the brown plastic of my in-tray. One of the scars that McDonald's had left on my heart was knowing that whenever you're employed, someone is making a lot more money out of having you than you are making. Perhaps that's what employment is. I felt that there were things purposefully hidden from my view. I had seen Big Nathan's daughter, who was sixteen and sometimes came in to shred all the documents at the back, and I had seen her iPod and nice jeans and I knew that it was all bought for her by us. It wasn't that I was jealous of her, even though I couldn't afford those things for myself, but more that it was evidence of where the money I was making for Big Nathan went. How utterly futile.

I looked at my empty tray, fearful that I must have somehow inadvertently done more than I'd been asked.

I went over to Ian, who brought me all the agreements each morning.

He was about a foot shorter than me and had just had his hair shaved right up the back, so in his shirt and tie he looked like a school boy. His coffee mug said *I'm just a shy guy with a big dick* and he drank about twenty cups a day.

"Hello," he said, without stopping typing.

"You got any more agreements for me?"

He kept typing.

"Ian?"

"Not today, no."

"You going out for a ciggie?" He was the only other smoker in the office apart from me, Rachel and Young Nathan, and I had seen him going out every day at eleven and three.

"Later," he said, unusually terse.

I spent the next hour sorting out my desk drawers.

I found quite a few old transmittal forms, which I dated and filed, and also about twenty tiny Post-it pads, which I gathered together in a little chunk and put flush against the drawer front. I gathered all the pens and tested them, until I had a paper with loads of little spirals on it.

Then I got a cloth from the kitchen and wiped down the desk, getting rid of all the dust and coffee rings and old paperclips.

I had three in-trays, stacked on top of each other at the edge of the desk. Even though they were empty now, they had always made me feel as if I was surrounded by piles of work, like a kitchen porter in a cartoon, so I decided to take out the poles between them and lay them out side by side. The difference in light was extraordinary, and I now had the illusion that each day it was up to me to choose what I did. I tucked the little poles away in the drawer.

Kim walked by, on her way up the back. "How are you?"

"Bored," I said.

"You got no agreements?"

Obviously not. "Nope."

"Any transmittal forms to file?"

"Nope. How's you?"

She rubbed the bump. "Starting to get tired really quickly. I can't sleep properly at all. I thought I was going to love it, this whole time of waiting and preparing before the baby comes, but I actually hate it."

"I'm glad you're not a marketing rep for pregnancy," I said. "No one would ever want to reproduce."

She smiled slightly. "Hmm. When are you going to start having babies, then?"

"I don't know." I wanted to hide my surprise. "Not yet."

She tipped her head on one side. "Better start soon."

"I'm only twenty-four."

"Prime baby age."

In my head I was screaming. "Do you think?"

"Hmm. Anyway, I like what you've done with your desk. Good to make it your own."

I started on the post.

RTW left and a minute later Ian went out for a fag. When he came back in he went to the kitchen and got an orange, and then I watched as he tried to cut into it with a blade the size of a bread knife.

"Do you think you've got a big enough knife there?" I called across from the pigeonholes.

He didn't look up from his hacking, made more awkward by the fact he was slumped in his chair and refused to lean forward. He said, "Just about, ta."

"Here, I've got a cleaver somewhere," I went on, turning away.

I could hear him laughing, and I realised it was the first time in a long time I had said something that even resembled a joke.

Waiting for the train felt endless. Helmet Man had a new coat, a creaky leather jacket which I wasn't sure suited him. Reading Woman was the same as always.

When I got home the Traffic Warden was in the flat's doorway, spoon in mouth and yoghurt in hand, frowning at the ceiling.

"They're at it again."

He meant the guys in the upstairs flat, Dusty and Jason, who'd been playing loud music a lot since they'd moved in. I didn't mind it too much, but I had headphones, big ones like cups over the ears, so I could block out the world at will.

Later we were watching a film when the Traffic Warden got up suddenly and thumped the ceiling, shouting through it. "You cunts! I'm gonna cut my fucking ears off in a minute!"

I smiled.

He'd always had this sort of total and absolute anger, a certainty that someone else was wrong and he was right. When we were students it would scare our housemates when he exploded over minor things, but never me. There was something slightly comical about it, but also a passion that I quite liked.

"Why don't you just go up there?"

"I will, if it goes on."

He sat back down on the sofa, folded his arms and glowered at the telly.

*

Ruth gave me some agreements to file and I waited until exactly 15.15 before I went up the back to do them. I had done five when I kicked my shoes off and squinted at my feet. The purple toenail was gone.

"Feet still there?" It was Young Nathan.

He started filing alongside me.

57

"How's it going?" I asked.

"I'm okay, thanks, and you?"

He was quite posh.

"I'm okay." I pulled a packed lever arch folder from the shelf and the contents collapsed out onto the floor, so I was left holding the cardboard by its finger hole. "Can I change that to 'I've been better'?"

He sniggered and so did I, sitting down so I could order the fallen papers before putting them back in the folder.

"How long have you been working here?" I asked him.

"Since June."

"Oh, okay, so not much longer than me, then."

"No. Did you know we graduated from the same uni?" he asked.

"Really? How did you know that?"

"Mary told me."

"What did you study?"

"English and French."

I stopped filing and so did he. "Are you fluent in French, then?"

"Yeah, I spent a year in France. You?"

"No."

"No what?"

"I don't speak French."

"I meant, what did you study?"

"Oh. English too, actually." I started filing again.

"Ah, okay. Makes sense."

"Why? Do I look booky or something?"

"No. Well, yeah, actually. A bit."

"Yes, and you."

"Weird we never met, though."

"Yeah."

We filed in silence for a bit. I finished putting the folder back together and slid it back onto the shelf.

"So, have you got a life plan, then?" he asked.

"Yeah." I lowered my voice. "Get out of here."

He laughed.

"What about you?" I asked.

"Well, I'm working on a novel."

"Oh, right."

"I know what you're thinking—"

"I severely doubt that."

"Well, everyone else, then. It's a pipe dream. But I know. I know that I should have some sort of plan B, but I've got this job and I'm just going to see what happens."

I looked over the office. Ruth was on the phone, gesticulating. Kim was standing at the photocopier, hand on hip. "If anything."

*

"Secret Santa?" Kim asked, holding out an envelope of folded slips.

I'd been watching her making her way round the office with some dread as I had this knowing feeling that I was going to get someone from debt collection that I didn't know at all, and probably a bloke. For a woman there was always the cop-out clause of chocolate or candles.

I got Nick.

"Who've you got?" I asked Rachel.

She nodded towards Young Nathan. The office was so small you couldn't really talk about anyone.

"Aw, you're so lucky, that's a good one."

"Yeah, I know. I was worried I'd get..." and she nodded at Big

59

Nathan. "Who've you got?"

I showed her my piece of paper.

She read it and frowned. "Who's that?"

I mouthed at her, *The one in purple. Debt.*

"*Oh.* I thought that was—" and she mouthed *Matt.*

I whispered back. "No, he's the one in black."

"He's quite fit."

"Do you think?" I put my slip of paper saying *Nick* in the bin and carried on typing an agreement.

"Don't you?"

"I guess so. I don't know. I never thought about it."

Next to me, Ruth sighed heavily and started dialling a number.

"No? Well, you're happily in luuuuurve."

I pulled a face.

"I can tell," she said. "I'm a bit psychic. You two are made for each other."

*

It was already the start of December and I was wondering if I was the only person who noticed that although it was cold and the leaves had turned into crispy rolls and fallen to the ground, not a drop of rain had fallen since that storm. I was aware that I had been waiting for winter to arrive, but like all British seasons it had crept in without anyone realising.

The mornings were so beautiful that I looked forward to walking to the station with the ground sparkling under my office shoes. I loved the sharpness of the air in my mouth and the skeletal trees spread like veins on the clear sky.

It was such a contrast to the office with its repressive atmosphere, the grey dullness permeating me as soon as I stepped into the building so it was as if I'd never left.

It didn't help that every morning when she got in, Kim had started singing to Young Nathan. The first one was *Last Christmas*, then *Silent Night*, then *Deck the Halls*. I thought of that story about a kid in a chemistry exam who poked two pens into his eyes and slammed his head against the desk.

I decided that I would steal a new pen from the box up the back for every time I had to listen to it.

The day of *Santa Baby*, I stole three.

I started to eat my lunch outside, amongst the blackened trees and the frosty white grass in the green space down the road. Because of the phones, I was always alone, and sitting in the office while everyone carried on typing around me didn't feel like a break.

Sometimes when I'd finished my sandwiches but didn't feel like reading, I'd sit with my hands in my coat pockets, waiting for time to pass until I had to go back to work.

Sometimes I decided that there had to be another life out there, waiting for me to step into it like a new shoe. My life felt as if it didn't match me at all, as if I'd picked up the wrong one by accident. I'd arrived here by mistake, taken a wrong turning on the map. I imagined that I was a character in a video game, and there was a button for a trapdoor, to take me to the next level, somewhere else, anywhere else, and all I had to do was find it.

I looked at the cloudless sky and wondered if the season had been sent to us as a last reminder of beauty before a huge black storm gurgled out of the sea and swallowed us all whole.

Clive

I did almost my whole Christmas shop on the first Saturday of December.

I was looking for something to get the Traffic Warden's mum in Debenhams when I saw the dress. The skirt part was blue-green satin as deep as ink, with sparkly black netting over it, and the top was a black corset with ribbons crisscrossing the back.

I ran my hands underneath the net, to feel the smooth richness of the fabric.

A shop assistant in a cerise blouse approached me and asked if I wanted any help. I asked her where the changing rooms were, and then took one of the dresses in my size and rustled up the back, slowly closing the curtain behind me.

I peeled off my jeans and sweatshirt, even took off my socks and bra, and let down my hair before slipping the dress over my head. I had to twist it to get the zip up to the top, and then I sighed, tipped my shoulders back and turned to look in the full-length mirror.

My skin looked very pale next to the dark dress.

Rachel had asked me earlier that week if I thought I was going to marry the Traffic Warden. I said if he asked me I would say yes, but as soon as I said it I realised that I sounded as if I was sitting around like a damsel waiting for him to ask me.

This dress was the first one I'd ever seen that I would get married in, and I pulled a face like broken flowers that all brides seem to have and imagined the Traffic Warden standing next to me, the two of us in front of all our friends and family.

Man and wife. The phrase made me nauseous.

I tried to imagine what life would start with this dress, but nothing came.

When I got home, Clive was standing outside our flat door.

"Oh – hello. How are you?" I said as I climbed the hallway steps, my bags clustered around my legs.

"I'm fine," he said.

Clive was our letting agent and he'd come, after sending us an ominous letter a week previously, to "inspect" the flat. He had steel-grey hair and his sad eyes turned downwards at the corners like those of a Disney hound.

He had shown us this flat and dealt with all the paperwork, so we'd never actually met our landlord. I imagined him to be somewhat otherworldly, as all of my previous landlords had been peculiar. During my third year at university, I had come home from a late shift at work to find my landlady in my bed.

"Here." I got my keys out and went in, holding the door open for him with my foot.

He stepped inside and wiped his feet on the mat, even though I hadn't bothered. He was wearing pinstripe trousers, a blue and white stripy smart shirt, and a black and electric blue diagonally striped tie. Even the Traffic Warden would have baulked at three different sorts of stripes.

I put my bags on the sofa and stood with my arms folded, looking out the window at the courtyard, where nine new wheelie bins were lined up. "Do you want a cup of tea?"

"I better not." He pointed up by the window frame. "I can see where the mould's coming through there."

I followed him into the bedroom and when he saw the ceiling, he winced. "You should have rung."

"Well, we thought it was just the building. It was already there when we moved in, we could see that it had just been painted over, so it's really only bloomed through in the last few weeks. I did make a note of it on the inventory."

He touched the wall. "It is the building to an extent – but I can see some condensation on the windows there. You need to be wiping that off, opening the windows, that sort of thing."

"It's winter – we can't have the windows open too much or we'd lose all the heat."

"Have you been using the dehumidifier?"

"No."

"Well, you can have that on. A human breathes out a litre of moisture every hour. It'll fill up straight away. I mean, I know you're not responsible for the mould being there in the first place, but there are measures you should be taking to make it better."

I hated this sort of conversation as I couldn't be sure whether it was the landlord's responsibility or ours, but either way he had lots of our money that he could withhold if he felt like it.

"Sponge off what's there, and get some mould killer. Apart from anything else, it's not good for your health to be living like this."

I told him about the dripping tap in the kitchen and the stiff lock on the front door and he noted them down on his clipboard.

As he was going, he said, "Sixties, seventies buildings are usually bad for damp. I don't want you to lose your deposit, see. It happened to me once in London. I had this studio flat and the windows were drenched every morning, so I wiped them off with a towel every day. Still got charged. It's unfair."

I looked into his sad eyes and wondered if I could trust him. "Thanks for letting me know. I appreciate that."

He half-smiled.

"You got more inspections?"

"Yeah. I'll be looking at mould all day."

I spent the rest of the afternoon sponging the mould. The bedroom ceiling was the hardest part, as the mould killer I'd found under the sink was in a mist spray and it kept floating into my eyes. I caught myself head down and wiping my eyes as if I was crying, standing on an old stool like a statue on a pedestal.

The Traffic Warden's hair was sticking up at the front in a scoop when he got in from work. I could time his homecoming by clockwork at this point and had started on dinner.

"Hello, Tintin."

"Hello, cunt face. What you making?"

"Turkey something with couscous and dips and bread."

He was leafing through the post. I hadn't even noticed a delivery.

"How many tickets'd you give out today?"

"Seven. This is for you," he said, holding out a small white envelope. I wiped my hands on my jeans and opened it. It was a letter from the university asking me to fill out a questionnaire to tell them where I was and what I was doing.

I put it straight in the bin.

*

Sunday morning. We woke up, and I rolled on top of the Traffic Warden so he couldn't put the telly on, as he always did.

"Get off."

"No."

His chest hair tickled my ear.

"Let's do something," I said.

"Like what?"

"I don't know."

"Get off, Heffalump, you're squashing me."

"Thanks."

"Get off, then."

I rolled away, and he sat up and switched the TV on, instantly absorbed by it.

I sat in the sheets, rumpled from sleep, and picked one of my nails. I thought he might take pity on me, hug me after all and tell me that I was loved. And more interesting than TV.

"If you had the option to find out when you're going to die, would you do it?" I asked.

He sighed. "Probably not."

"No, I didn't think so."

"Would you?"

"Well, my first reflex was no, but I can't really see any downside to knowing."

"You wouldn't be able to live." He changed the channel.

"Of course you would. Suppose you find out it's in forty years' time, you could just relax, take it easy."

"What if it was next week?"

"You'd be able to… prepare."

"Prepare what? You're dying, not going on holiday."

"Spend all your money. Tell some people they're cunts. Tell some people you love them. Skip work."

"Are you still looking for other jobs?"

"Yeah."

*

Monday morning was almost insufferable.

The Traffic Warden had a day off and rang me on my mobile at

10.05. "There's ten more bags out there."

"What?"

"The rubbish. There's ten more bags of it, just dumped."

I gave a big sigh. Somehow bags had been piling up since we'd got the wheelie bins delivered. For the first few weeks the bin men had taken them, but the previous week they'd started sticking bright yellow labels over the tops and leaving them for the foxes to rip apart. "This is starting to border on unhealthy obsession. Why on earth have you rung to tell me that?"

"I'm just so *angry* about it, that's all."

"I can hear that, but what do you want me to do? If you're so bothered, do something about it yourself."

"I will. I just need some support."

"Oh, for God's sake."

I hung up and put the phone down with such force it skittered on the desk. I knew that he would ring his mother now.

Rachel was looking at me. "Everything all right?"

"Yeah." I sighed and sort of smiled.

"Men, eh?"

For some reason, I didn't want her to think it was bigger than it was, so I told her the bin story.

"Oh dear," she said.

"Sometimes I don't know if he's an old man or a child."

Rachel was going through a stack of papers, and licked her finger to get better purchase. "I know. They're just not *normal*."

Then Kim was given the task of putting up and decorating a plastic tree, and she chose the spot next to my desk. She kept sighing and groaning.

"How's it going?" she asked.

"Fine, thanks," I said. "You?"

She talked about the pregnancy at length while I tried not to drift off, though thankfully Rachel cut in when she started about incontinence. Then we both heard about the rocking chair she'd ordered off eBay, the Moses basket, and the colour of the paint for the nursery.

"Bet you can't wait, though," Rachel said, before she started on what pushchair she was going to get. "Must be exciting."

"Yeah, it is. It's hard, though, 'cause in a way I want her to hurry up and just come, but then again I hope she doesn't come before Christmas as I'll have to buy her a present."

In the afternoon Rachel and I got onto the topic of stuff we'd liked as kids.

"Who was your favourite Mr Man?" she asked.

"I don't know, really. I quite liked Mr Sneeze."

"What did he look like?"

"Sort of like a blue star. What about you?"

She answered without hesitation. "Mr Messy."

"Oh, yeah, he was the pink scribble."

"Yeah. And those two men in top hats came and combed him —"

"Until he was all smooth! I remember that one."

"I always thought it was a shame, the way they did that. He probably liked being just the way he was."

I smiled.

So did she. "I'm quite weird about stuff like that."

"Yeah, and me. I cried at Mr Bean. You know the Christmas special, where he has that girlfriend and buys her a picture hook instead of a ring?"

"I must admit, I always found Mr Bean very unsettling."

"Seriously? Everyone thinks I'm weird."

She frowned. "No, not at all. He elicits strange reactions from people. Honestly." She looked at something behind me and I followed her gaze to Kim, who was standing there, rubbing her bump.

"Oh, hi," I said.

"Are you free for a bit?" she asked.

"Um, yeah, I guess so."

"'Cause Big Nathan wanted me to show you submission before I go."

"Oh, right. Yeah, fine."

I dragged my chair over to her desk and she explained to me that there were three submissions in total: MRP, ICS, and CRS, and I was to do each of them every day at around three o'clock.

All it seemed to consist of was the same process of boxes to be okayed and exited, one after another. It seemed easy to forget which part of the process you were in, beginning or end, but it was as mindless as any other task. The whole time Kim was explaining it, she fiddled with her hair, winding it round and round her fingers.

"So how's the four-by-four working out?" I asked.

Young Nathan looked up and I could see he was listening.

"No one *ever* lets me out." She whined like a child. "No one likes a four-by-four, do they? Oh! Just remembered —" She pulled open the bottom drawer of her desk, and I could see that it was chock-full of old copies of *Closer* and *Heat*. "I can't be bothered to throw these out, so I'm leaving them here. If ever you want a magazine, just help yourself."

I knew I never would. "Thanks."

Afterwards, I went out for a cigarette with Young Nathan.

"How's the novel going?" I asked.

"Okay, thanks."

"What's it about?"

He sighed.

"Sorry, just curious."

"It's about working in an office," he said, scuffing the toes of his shoes on the ground.

"Does it help?" I asked.

He blew a smoke ring. "Well, it makes me feel we're not as insignificant as I know we really are, if that's what you mean."

"I'll take that. So tell me, what happens?"

"I don't know yet."

"You don't know?"

"I'm trying to decide between two options."

"What are they?"

We were silent for so long I wondered if he was going to speak.

"Well, either there'll be an apocalypse…"

"Right."

"Or nothing at all."

*

When I got to the flat the Traffic Warden wasn't at the door like usual, so I dug my key out and went in to find him absorbed in a video game.

I went to get changed as I couldn't bear being in my office clothes for any longer than I had to.

The Traffic Warden called through to me. "The bin situation has been sorted."

I'd forgotten all about it.

He pressed one button on the controller over and over. "I spoke to a man at the council. The waste man."

"Thank God for that – I was really panicked for a minute

there."

"Don't be a cunt."

"Don't call me at work again about pointless rubbish."

I went over to him and sat, waiting for him to pause the game. It took a while but when he did we nuzzled and played with each other like animals, each of us pretending to bite the other's neck. It would have looked peculiar from the outside but it made sense to us.

I sat by the window in the deckchair and lit a cigarette. It was already dark but due to the Christmas lights on the house opposite I could make out Mini Man and his moody girlfriend, both sitting on the wall smoking.

Mike was talking to them. I was tempted to open the window so I could hear what they were saying, but it was too cold for that.

A car turned into our parking area. Someone in a white tunic was driving.

I wondered about the old woman downstairs. She must have felt like she was living in a prison. In some Inuit cultures, when people get to a certain age everyone gathers and they put them on a raft of ice and let them float away. When I first heard it I thought it was totally barbaric, but now more and more it seemed like the only right thing to do.

Or maybe there was no right thing when it came to death. It seemed stupid to even speak about death when you were in your twenties.

I looked at Mike's belly, at his strange head. Only wisps of grey hair remained, so you could see the shape of his skull, and all his liver spots. Would he be sorry to die? Would anyone be sorry to see him go? Did he feel abandoned?

"What?" the Traffic Warden asked.

71

I turned around and the deckchair creaked. "What's what?"

"I thought you said something."

"No."

*

I watched the Traffic Warden scrutinise the bed and surrounding area for spiders.

"Can you get up a sec?" he asked.

"What? Why?"

"I just thought I saw a spider run towards you."

"Don't be silly, it was probably just a bit of fluff or something. Get in bed, will you?"

"Please."

"For God's sake." But I got up.

He pinched at something on the sheet. "Got it!"

"What was it?"

He flicked it away. "Fluff."

We both got into bed and wrestled with the duvet for a bit, before I turned off the lamp and rested my head on his shoulder. I felt his hand rubbing my side, and I ran my feet up his hairy legs. He started to grope around my breasts.

"No."

"Oh, come on."

"No, I don't really want to."

He sighed.

Car lights flashed across the ceiling.

"Hey, look, I don't mean to scare you but I saw a tarantula earlier." I started climbing my hand over his shoulder, moving as I thought a tarantula would. "I think it's still loose somewhere."

The soft vibration of his laughter came up my fingers before I heard it. "Go to sleep, you mong."

I rolled away, far too awake for sleep.

The ceiling flashed again.

His breathing got heavier and deeper and he began to snore.

I turned over, tugging the duvet with me, and the Traffic Warden let out a low moan. I switched on the side lamp to read. The book was about a lonely woman who found a partner but was discovering that he wasn't quite right. The narrator kept saying, *Life is sad. Here is someone*, until I didn't know how much more of the book I could take.

I can still remember the moment I first fell in love with the Traffic Warden.

We were friends, living in a big dirty house with four other students, and he had the box room, which was so small that he kept most of his clothes in the hallway in bin liners.

One time I got back from McDonald's and I went straight up to see him for a chat. I sat on his bed in my uniform and we smoked and watched his miniscule telly and he moaned about how I smelt of chip fat and told me about how he thought I was a suck-up, goody-two-shoes sort of worker. I said he smelt of cheap beer and was a lazy waste of space.

Before I knew it, two hours had passed, and as I went to go he switched off the TV and began fiddling about with a CD. I'd just climbed over his clothes in the hallway when I heard the opening bars of the Depeche Mode song *Stripped*.

Maybe it was the engine noise that made me stop still or maybe it was the first line, but whatever it was, I stood at the top of the stairs listening to the whole song, convinced that he was playing it just for me.

The song was about knowing someone, not their face or clothes or even who they thought they were, but knowing all the worst, most awkward and embarrassing bits, and not only knowing them but *wanting* them.

I felt that he wanted truth over beauty or anything else, and that was the moment.

My parents were good friends too.

My mum saw my dad walking down the road with a pint of milk and a hole in his jumper and thought he needed looking after, and then they met at a party a few days later and they've barely spent a night apart since.

My dad proposed after nine days, and my mum accepted. They were married half a year later, two months after Charles and Diana. When she told me this, I was sitting on our kitchen table in my school uniform, twelve years old.

"But you can't have loved him. Why did you say *yes*?" I asked her.

"Oh, I don't know. His scrambled eggs, probably. He fell in love with Bongo first, anyway."

Bongo was a golden retriever, and Mum had bought her as a puppy. I was only about four when she died but I remember us all going for a walk to the estuary, which was full of green slime and stank of mud.

It must have been a combination of Bongo being so old and us going too far, but when we were on the way home she couldn't jump the rocks, so my dad, lifter of anything heavy, picked her up to carry her back to the car. I wonder how much my mum loved my dad on that day, as he clambered across slippery rocks with this huge golden dog in his arms, his wax jacket streaked with mud from her claws and fronds.

I never saw my mum cry so much as when the dog died.

I looked at the Traffic Warden as he slept and wondered if he would do a thing like that.

He groaned again and I turned off the light and lay awake.

It felt like a long time. I listened to some drunk people walking past outside, the clop of two pairs of heels getting closer and then a shriek.

For some reason, I whispered, "Are you asleep?"

"Yes."

"Do you think there's really anything more to love than lying down in a dark room next to someone every night?" I asked.

"Do you think there's anything more annoying than being asked stupid questions when you're trying to sleep?"

"How do I know that it's not all pretend and you don't really love me?"

"I am pretending."

I smiled into the dark.

"Sleep now."

Erica

On Monday morning, Ian brought over a large fresh batch of agreements and added them to a stack which had been getting a bit taller each day.

"Piling up," he said, taking a sip out of his *Shy Guy* coffee mug. His hair had grown slightly so he no longer looked like a school boy. "You're going to need a new in-tray at this rate."

"I don't know why," I said. "I'm going as fast as I can." I knew that submission took a little chunk out of my afternoon, but I didn't want it to be taken away from me as it helped to break up the day.

"Oh, yes, I know. I checked your numbers yesterday."

"My numbers?"

"Yeah. You do about a hundred and seventy a day."

"Oh, right." I felt almost robbed, but I wasn't sure of what exactly. "Is that good?"

"Yeah, it's very good." He took another sip of coffee. "Exactly the same as Mel, in fact."

I was looking out the window and watching the AquAid man unload barrels of water for the office above us when I realised that Mary was standing by my desk, holding a yellow folder. She put it on my desk and slid it towards me.

She whispered, "Kim's leaving card."

"Oh, right. Okay."

"Will you pass it round customer services when you're done?"

"Of course."

When Mary had gone I opened up the folder. The card had a picture of a teddy bear crying and said *Sorry You're Leaving* in big red bubble letters across the top.

It'd already been round debt collection, and Big Nathan and Mark had seen it, so a lot of the usual comments were taken. *Good luck. Best wishes.*

Rachel was on the phone, so I wrote a note on my telephone pad. *What do you put in someone's card when you don't like them?!*

And she wrote back, *FUCK OFF!*

I smiled.

In the end I plumped for, *Best wishes for the future and hope everything goes well with the baby xx.*

When Rachel got off the phone she asked, "Do you want to go out for a drink on Thursday?"

"Yeah, sure. How come? Where's Amy?"

"She's going to stay at my mum's."

"Oh, right. Yeah, that'd be good."

My phone went, and it was an old woman. She wouldn't tell me who she was, but asked for Rachel.

I put her on mute. "Rach, some crackpot for you."

"Is it an old woman?" Then her phone started ringing.

"Yeah."

"Oh, I need to take that call."

"Here." I gave her my handset and took it off mute, and as she started speaking I reached across and answered her phone and put that call through to Kyle, before untangling the cat's cradle of curly wires to put her handset back.

In the afternoon, I always had some post to send out, and I was sorting by the pigeonholes when Erica came by. She was small and pale, with eyes that bulged like a frightened horse's. I always thought we would get on if we just spoke to each other, but somehow we never had.

She sat with the debt collection lot but she wasn't credit control because she didn't take phones, and now she had a pile of sheets in her arms and was putting them into their correct pigeonholes.

"What is it you do?" I asked.

She looked at me as if she was terrified, and I suddenly realised how dark the pigeonholes were because I could see the whites of her eyes. She almost whispered it. "Tracings."

I had no idea what that meant, but I didn't want to ask her anything else. "Oh, right."

That night the Traffic Warden and I wrapped Christmas presents and watched an old episode of *Star Trek*. To be fair I was mostly wrapping; he just cut strips of tape when he wasn't at the telly.

I like wrapping presents.

There's something satisfying about it, even though you're building up the anticipation for something that will get a lukewarm reaction at best if it's given to anyone over the age of ten. Past the age of ten there probably aren't many genuine surprises left.

"I'm going out with Rachel on Thursday night."

He didn't take his eyes off the screen. "What for?"

"Hot sex."

He said nothing.

"Tape, please." He cut a bit and then I pulled it off the table. It was brown with flakes of wood. "No, we're going out for a few drinks."

"Where're you gonna go?"

"I don't know. They're all the same up there, aren't they?"

Up the road from our offices were more offices, much bigger

than ours, mostly for banks and insurance and equally dull things. Beyond that, there were a couple of shops and four bars, two on each side of the road. One of them was always changing its name or refurbishing to look more like the others, to the point where all that was between them were minute differences in colour schemes and the strength of the patio heaters.

"Don't go to Orange Square."

"Why?"

"It's dodgy."

"Don't be silly."

"It is. It's full of drug dealers and gangsters."

"Don't be ridiculous."

"Has that Kim woman left yet?"

I had told him about her in snippets. "Her last day is on Friday."

Star Trek seemed like one senseless conversation after another, and I said so.

"Sci-fi can tell you more about humanity then you realise."

"I don't see how aliens can tell us more about ourselves than human actors in situations on Earth."

"Well, they can."

"Like what? Actually, don't answer that. It's almost a moot point, because they're all human anyway."

"Well, yeah, the actors are human."

"Obviously, but they're meant to be from other planets, and they've all got human faces, just slightly warped."

"Yeah, so?"

"*So*, the reason we are the way we are is evolution, right? So why would a creature in another galaxy evolve exactly like us, only with ridges on their nose or whatever? It doesn't make sense. I mean, what are the chances of another planet being *that* similar to ours? Is the imagination really that small?"

"You think too much."

"Yeah? And that guy looks a bit like you."

"Worf?"

"Yeah."

"That's a coincidence, because he's sex on legs."

There was some sort of battle on a spaceship with cardboard-sprayed-silver blades and I started giggling.

The Traffic Warden sighed. "Come on, this is classic."

"You only think it's good 'cause you liked it when you were a kid."

"No, it really is great."

"No, it really is *shite*. More tape, please."

*

At five o'clock on Thursday, Rachel stood up and wrapped her scarf round and round her neck. "So, where d'you wanna go, mate?" she asked.

"I really don't mind."

"Orange Square?"

I smiled. "Sure."

"I'll get the first ones," Rachel said. She was already leaning against the bar with her purse, so there didn't seem much point in arguing.

"Thanks," I said. "Shall we sit outside?" They'd stopped smoking in pubs five months previously, but I still wasn't used to it and grumbled about it like an old man.

"Yeah, I need to smoke."

I craned to see out the window. "I wonder where all the drug dealers and gangsters are," I said. I had told her about the Traffic Warden's comment at the office and she'd laughed.

80

"Hiding from us. There are some grubby people around here, though. I was in here with my sister ages ago, and this horrible man put his hand on my back. I said, 'Get off unless you wanna pay for that.' I was wearing something backless, but eurgh, I'm not having him touching me up."

I'd never worn anything backless in my life, but when I was with Rachel I felt as if I might have done.

When we sat down, she said, "Right, so what do you *really* think of everybody at work?"

We smoked fag after fag while the office workers drifted up the hill. I watched them as if they were part of a nature documentary about migrating birds. As if I never walked amongst them.

Rachel clapped her hands. "Okay, okay – I know this is a pointless question for you, but if you had to have sex with one person at the office, who would it be?"

"What, a meaningless fuck? I don't know."

"Come on."

"Matt in debt collection, maybe?"

Rachel tapped her fag on the ashtray. "Which one?"

"Oh, you know – the guy who always wears black shirts. You said he was good-looking."

"Oh, I know! Yeah, he is sexy."

"I know. I'll tell you what really did it for me, though – okay, this sounds really geeky now, but he's really *smart*. Every time I put a call through to him, I say, like, 'Janine Clarke for you,' and he always says to put her straight through, he knows the reference number and everything. And he sounds kind of sinister, you know?"

"Yeah, he does. Fucking hell, if I had debts and Matt rang me up I'd pay them straight away."

"Yeah, and me. What about you, who would you have sex with?"

"I don't know... Matt's probably sexiest. There's not a lot of talent at Weblands, is there, really?"

"One of the many things it lacks."

"I'll tell you something, though. Once I was filing some agreements—"

"*You*, filing?"

Rachel's filing had been stacking up in her filing tray, and it was now approaching six inches in height.

"Yeah, it was ages ago. Anyway, I was filing, and I looked up and caught Nathan's eye, and I don't know why but I actually *blushed*."

"I can't imagine you blushing."

"I know."

"Is this a confession, then? Are you telling me you've secretly been in love with your Secret Santa?"

"No, not Young Nathan." She stabbed her fag into the centre of the aluminium tray on the table and blew out the last drag. "Big Nathan."

After it got too cold to sit outside, we went back to her flat, stopping in the off-licence on the way. Walking around lines of bottles glinting in the light made me feel really hammered, but I didn't mind because Rachel was too.

She barely glanced at the shelves, but went straight to the counter and asked the guy behind it for two bottles of the driest white wine they had.

Her flat was how I'd thought it would be: small, clinically neat, with wooden floors and photos of Amy and a box of pink plastic toys in the corner.

She gave me a tour of the whole place, including Amy's room, which was pink and small. Rachel sat on the bed and I looked at a dresser covered in dolls. "I miss her," she said. "Even for one night."

"I bet." I couldn't really understand how you could miss something you saw every day.

"I love her so much. You know, I can't recommend having kids highly enough. I know how stupid this sounds, but I felt like I loved Amy even before I had her. I sound mental, don't I? When are you having kids?"

I shrugged. "Not yet."

The highlight of the tour was a cupboard in which she stored two hundred pairs of shoes, still in their boxes.

"Okay, *now* I think you're fucking mental."

"Do you want to see my favourite pair?" she asked.

"If you really want me to, but don't expect a great reaction. I'm really not a shoe person."

The favourite pair were pink snakeskin heels and she squeaked as she got them out, and stroked the leather. "Oh, I just love them! Aren't they great?"

"Um, not my cup of tea. Him indoors says I walk like a pirate in high heels. He calls me Jack Sparrow."

"Oh, he doesn't! That's really mean."

"No, he's just taking the piss. And he's kind of right."

"You just need to *practise*."

"Hmmm. I can't see it." I wanted to change the subject. "How on earth do you afford all these shoes?"

"Beg, borrow and steal."

We both stood for a minute, looking at all the boxes.

"Shall we have a fag?" I asked.

"Yes, let's. Just need the loo."

I went downstairs and gazed along her bookshelves. There were a lot of pastel paperbacks about flailing singletons and new mums, but amongst them were fat copies of *Foucault's Pendulum* and *The Interpretation of Murder*. They seemed like opposing forces but suited Rachel somehow.

I pulled out a big hardback about eyebrows, which was full of black-and-white pictures of old film stars. I started to wonder if women's physical differences had been tolerated more back then. Greta Garbo wasn't conventionally beautiful at all, but there was undoubtedly something striking about her face. She'd never have been able to consider a modelling career if she'd been born when I had.

I heard Rachel's feet on the stairs and then felt her looking at the book over my shoulder.

"You look a bit like Grace Kelly," I said. "Don't you think?"

"Thanks, hun, but I think that's something of an exaggeration."

"Beauty's such a funny thing, don't you think?"

"Yeah. It's fascinating, though."

"Okay, if you could choose, would you rather be more beautiful, or more intelligent?"

She tucked her chestnut hair behind her ear. "More beautiful."

"Seriously?"

"Yeah. Never underestimate the power of your own beauty. You can get anything you want out of life."

"*You* could. *I* couldn't."

"Of course you could."

We went out to her balcony and lit up. She gave me a long look.

"Tell me a secret," I said in the darkness.

She had her arms folded across her chest. "You've got to swear not to tell anyone." She blew smoke out of her nose.

"I won't."

"Please."

"I promise. Who the fuck would I tell?"

She took a deep breath. "A very long time ago, before Amy was born, I was once crowned Miss United Kingdom."

"Oh."

"I know."

"Seriously?"

"Yeah."

"Well, your secret's safe with me."

"Thanks. I'm not exactly ashamed, I just – well, I don't know, it's not something that I want everyone to know."

"No, I guess not. What did it feel like?"

"What?"

"To be crowned."

"It was pretty weird. I was young – I mean, I was only eighteen, so I didn't really understand it, but it didn't feel like all the dreams I'd had. You know, it was meant to be this incredible moment, and it was nothing like how I thought it would be."

I looked at her high cheekbones and dark bob and smiled. "Wow. I'm standing with the most beautiful girl in the UK."

She pouted. "Please don't."

There was an awkward moment.

"Sorry," she said.

"What's up?"

She looked at me and even in the dark I could see her eyes glistening. "It was such a horrible experience." She paused and I watched smoke unfurling from her nostrils. "I was being told that I was the most beautiful girl in the country, but I didn't realise until afterwards that it was never on *my* terms, it was always on someone else's. And it was never going to be enough."

"But you said you'd choose to be beautiful over smart."

"I know."

Bobby

The next day, I went into the Londis between the station and the office to buy some Lucozade for my hangover. The shop was a strange place. To begin with it was so overstocked that I spent most of my time in there squeezing past people and trying not to send hundreds of packets skittering across the floor. Everything in the shop was tailored towards commuters, like prawn sandwiches and individual tins of beer, crisps and fags and Anadin.

I got two bags of humbugs as well as the Lucozade, and was served by a guy who was at least six foot five and shaped like a barrel. His short dark hair was on end and he served from a raised platform behind the cashier desk, so I felt like I was being served by a slow King Kong.

"Hello, Madam," he said. He had a slight lisp.

"Hello," I said, as he stooped over my bottles to beep them through. He did this by rocking back and forth, almost mechanically, like one of those wooden birds that drink water. I just stood and watched a patch of dark dribble on his chest, just next to his name badge. *Bobby.*

He waved one of my bottles in front of the machine and he must have missed the bar code because there was no beep, but I didn't say anything and he kept rocking.

I handed him the money. He said, "Thank you, Madam."

Some kids behind me in the queue started giggling behind their hands.

It was Kim's last day at Weblands. She sang Young Nathan an

extra-long song in the morning, *All I Want for Christmas Is You*, and I made a mental note to steal a hole punch when I was less hungover.

After lunch, I thought about how Weblands was a very steady control for experiment. For a long time I had been tempted to start altering different variables, just to see what changes rippled out.

Occasionally Ruth or Ian would hand me a piece of paper and tell me to enter it in the system, and I couldn't help but wonder what would happen if I just lost it without reading it, if I slipped it into the space between my desk and Rachel's.

At 15.24, my phone rang. I could see from the extension number that it was Big Nathan.

I picked it up and said my usual spiel, pretending I didn't know it was him.

"Are you doing submission?"

"Sorry. I'll do it now."

I looked over and saw him smile and run his fingers down his tie. "Okay."

When I went across the office Kim was still at her desk, banging her drawers open and shut to empty them.

"Sorry," I said. "I need to do submission."

"Can't you wait a minute? It's my last day and I've got loads to get through." She sounded breathless.

"Okay."

Young Nathan raised his eyebrows, but didn't say anything.

When Kim had moved over to accounts and I could finally start submission, Young Nathan said, "You're a bit late."

I tried to think of something funny in reply, but my head was pounding.

Mary leaned over. "Better late than never."

"Uh, Mary," Big Nathan called over, "can you fetch me a C5 envelope from up the back, please?"

She smiled and asked, "Window or non-window?"

"Window. Thank you."

I watched her go, and wondered how it was that Big Nathan didn't find it embarrassing to ask for such trivial tasks to be carried out by other people.

After every submission, I had to print out and hand him a little chunk of submission reports, and I'd noticed that, in addition to sending her up the back for stationery, he made Mary file them. It was a job that took no longer than one minute, but he never did it himself. I didn't know if it was ridiculous or sinister.

Submission was nothing to do with her at all.

Ian was on the phone, sipping coffee and leaning so far back in his chair that he was looking at the ceiling.

I whispered to Young Nathan, "I dare you to pull on Ian's gas lift."

He smiled but shook his head.

I looked around, at all the calm people typing. "Do you ever think about wreaking havoc in this place?"

He continued to tap away at his keyboard, glaring into his screen, and I continued to write dates in the column on the submission sheet.

"Think about it. Lost agreements. Shredded documents. Wrong dates. Misplaced files."

He succumbed. "Calls diverted."

"Exactly. I could create absolute chaos. That's an unspeakable power, if you think about it."

I wondered if Big Nathan was listening to us and I added, "Of course I would never do it."

Ian finished on the phone. "You're coming to the Christmas party, aren't you?"

It was being held the weekend before Christmas and Kim had already organised it, despite the fact she would be extremely pregnant by then. She'd given me an invite when I'd very first started and since then I'd been thinking of what possible excuse I could give to get out of it.

"I can't come," I said. "I've got to go see my parents that weekend 'cause I'm not seeing them at Christmas." A rock-solid excuse, by anyone's standards.

"Oh, you're joking," Ian said. "Well, you'll miss out on the free wine." They were going for a sit-down meal at some golf club or something, and there was a rumour about bottles of wine on each table.

"More for the rest of you, then."

"And you'll miss Secret Santa."

We were to leave our Secret Santa presents under the office tree with an envelope label to say who it was for, and they were going to be opened at the Christmas do. So far there was only one under there, so it was obviously from Kim.

"Hey, who've you got?" I asked Ian.

"Can't say, it's secret."

"Oh, come on."

He leaned across and whispered that it was Kelly. "I'm totally stuck. I've no idea what to get."

"I don't know what to get mine either."

"Who've you got?"

I mouthed *Nick*.

"That's easy, just get something football."

"I don't know anything about football. Wanna swap?"

Young Nathan looked up. "No swapping allowed."

"Yeah, all right, then," Ian said. "Done."

"Good." I turned to Young Nathan. "Who've you got, anyway?"

"Secret."

"Be quiet."

"*Secret* Santa. It's a secret."

Mary leaned over and whispered, "Gather round Kim's desk at half four."

I nodded. "Okay."

"You've signed the card, haven't you?"

"Yeah."

I knew from when Mel had left that this would be another strange display, where everyone stood around and watched as Big Nathan gave her a leaving card and present. Earlier in the week I had caught Mary wrapping Kim's present behind the file shelves up the back.

It was a jungle-themed play mat for the baby, red and green and purple and yellow, and we all stood round and watched her unwrap it. There was a muted spatter of applause.

"Thanks, everyone," she said, swinging her hair over her shoulder. "I'm sure little Tinkerbell will *love* it."

Later, I overheard a mistake in the system. Kyle called over to Ruth, saying that an agreement was missing, when he needed to send the client a copy.

"Just phone the club and ask them to fax theirs over," Ruth said.

They didn't have it either.

Kelly

When it came to buying Kelly's Secret Santa I was more stuck than I'd thought I would be and suddenly saw why Ian had been so keen to trade. She was seventeen and resolutely unenthusiastic about *everything*, regarding the whole office through docile, elephant-grey eyes as if she'd already lived there for a hundred years. Perhaps we should have had a lot in common, but we didn't.

The only presents I was good at choosing were books, but when I tried to casually probe her about what she'd read recently, she told me that she'd only ever read one book.

"What was it?"

"Dunno. *Of Mice and Men* or something in school. It was crap."

I was only seven years older than her, but I felt like I was talking to my grandchild.

"Don't you feel like you're missing out, though?"

"No. Don't like reading."

In the end I bought a pair of silver hoop earrings from Topshop and some chocolate, wrapped it up in gold paper and as soon as she went to frank the post one day I stuck a label on it and put it under the tree, knowing that she would hate it and hoping she'd never, ever know it was me.

After I'd done my part, I started wondering who'd got me and decided through some vague intuition that it might be Kelly, until a week or so later a present with my name appeared under the tree and I saw that it was book-shaped.

"How many tickets'd you give out today?"

"Six."

"Only six?"

"Yeah."

I sat in the deckchair, lit a cigarette and watched Mike walking back and forth along the front wall, every now and then stooping to pick something up like a chicken in a farmyard.

"Did Rachel smoke when she was pregnant?" The Traffic Warden had been fascinated by her since I'd gone for the drink.

"Yeah," I said.

"Really?"

"Yeah."

"You'd better not do that."

"Oh, yeah? Why don't you shit a fridge and then tell me that again?"

"I'm serious. You better not do that to our child. If you do—"

I looked at him with raised eyebrows but he stopped. "Oh, please tell me, what is the end of that sentence?"

"You know what I mean."

"What I know is that it really disturbs me that you think you can just lay down the law and I'll fall in line and obey. Women are meant to be liberated these days, you know."

He leaned over to see out the window. "What the *fuck* is Mike doing?"

I suddenly realised, but as if I'd known all along, I said, "Picking up fag butts."

Henri Lloyd

As a gesture of goodwill, Big Nathan gave us all Christmas Eve off, as well as Christmas Day and Boxing Day, and as the twenty-fifth fell on a Tuesday we all had a five-day break.

On the Tuesday before Christmas, I left the office and was walking down the hill to the station when I passed a fat, short guy in a brown mac who'd stopped in the middle of the pavement and was staring, open-mouthed, at the Londis on the other side of the street.

He seemed so oblivious to all of the suits as they spilled around him that I almost found myself saying hello, but he looked too spaced out even for me. As I passed him I saw he had *Henri Lloyd* embroidered onto his bag in dirty white thread, the name of the company that had made it.

When I got to the platform I started thinking about the various ways that people would spend their Christmases.

Reading Woman looked like she had a family, and I guessed at two kids, perhaps grown up. I was mentally guessing their ages when she looked up from her book and into my face, and I turned away, embarrassed.

Helmet Man was easier to imagine, as with the days passing and him always turning up in clean trousers I had revised my madman opinion of him and now believed the truth to be far more mundane. I pictured a wife and a young child or baby called Oliver or Lucas.

I thought Henri Lloyd had a carer or an elderly mother, and would probably spend his Christmas in a house silent apart from a ticking clock.

I didn't see Henri Lloyd on the platform but he must have got on my train as I saw him at the other end, climbing the dirty station steps to the exit one at a time, like a child. With all the suits rushing around him he looked like a snail stuck in a swarm of ants.

*

On Christmas Day the sky was bright blue. The kitchen floor was freezing when I made the morning tea and took it to the Traffic Warden.

"Presents!" I dropped three neatly wrapped packages on the bed: a long *Doctor Who* style scarf that I'd knitted secretly while he worked at the weekends, a big map of the world for the wall, and three novels that I thought he'd like.

I opened my Secret Santa from work, and the book-shaped gift turned out to be a small hardback called *1000 Books to Read Before You Die*.

After we got dressed, we went to his family's house, as they lived just down the road. I'd never been much of a one to fuss about Christmas and nor had my family, but I texted my mum. I got the feeling that the Traffic Warden's mum would have been a bit heartbroken if he'd chosen to spend Christmas anywhere other than with his family.

His entire family consisted of his parents and his sister, his aunt and her husband and their three children, and his maternal grandparents. They all got together every Christmas. His grandparents were both compos mentis and active despite their age and his parents were kind and welcoming, so much so that I felt as if none of them had ever been touched by pain.

Whenever I had taken friends, and later boyfriends, to meet my parents, I'd felt that I had to give a warning, a sort of disclaimer so afterwards I could say, *I did warn you.* My parents were not cruel, or unwelcoming; just weird.

I knew from the instant that I met his mother that the Traffic Warden had never had to do that.

The spread that the Traffic Warden's mum put on was extraordinary. There was both turkey and ham, a hundred and one potatoes, parsnips, carrots, cabbage, swede, Brussels, two different kinds of stuffing, pigs in blankets and cheese in blankets, and Yorkshires. I thought when he came to mine for Christmas he'd be very disappointed.

They pulled crackers before the meal and all put on the paper crowns. I couldn't bear the feeling of it on my head, like something that was half there and half not, so I refused to wear it.

The youngest cousin kept trying to put it on me and I kept taking it off. I didn't care that I was on my own. Perhaps something inside me wanted to spoil it, to make it awkward.

"You *have* to wear it," she said.

"No, I don't."

"It's Christmas."

"I don't care if it's the apocalypse. I'm not wearing it."

My mum usually picked me up a few things each year, like second-hand books, a jumper, and a few jokes. We made an effort to be irreverent: she bought me a tin of plasters that were covered in neon pictures of Christ, and I gave her a calendar I found on the internet, with a different Roman Catholic priest for every month.

I had never believed in Santa and stopped getting a stocking when I was about ten, which I hadn't lamented. The day came with the revelation that Traffic Warden still had one, and also that he'd been bought every item on his Christmas list. There was so much stuff exchanged that it took all afternoon to unwrap presents and by the end I'd started to feel a bit sick.

His parents spoiled me too, giving me fluffy socks and Brazil nut body butter and a mug that was designed like one of Penguin's famous classic book covers. His mum had chosen Virginia Woolf, *A Room of One's Own*. I didn't know what to do with myself.

"Do you like her?" she asked.

I smiled. I supposed I seemed like the sort of person who would. "Actually, I've never read her. But I will now."

The best of the presents was a book called *Pick Me Up*, which was a trivia book aimed at children. It was the sort of book that you grow up with, and look at when you're six and see some things, and then different things when you're seven and so on. When you're a young teen you barely glance at it, and then you're packing up your stuff to move out, and you find it and its worn pages and look back and remember all the things you used to think about the world and the way it was.

After the great present-opening ceremony, I sat on the sofa with a glass of ice and amaretto and the book, and flicked it open to a double-page spread of two photos of a young woman's face. They looked identical at first glance, but then it became obvious that the one on the left was slightly more freckly. There were pores, and a stray eyebrow hair, and tiny hairs on her upper lip. The one on the right had none of these things.

As soon as I saw it I knew that I would keep the book for my children, for those two pictures alone.

The Traffic Warden's grandparents lived even closer to us than his parents and we walked back with them at the end of the day, slipping about on the frosty pavement, all of us a bit drunk.

They walked ahead, arm in arm, and I wondered if we would ever be like that, walking with our grandchild and their partner on Christmas Day.

After we said goodbye to them, I asked the Traffic Warden if he felt lucky.

He thought for a long minute and then said, "No, not really."

"Are you serious?"

"Yeah, why?"

I realised then that I'd made a fist in my pocket. "No reason."

When we got in, the Traffic Warden switched on the Xbox and I put on some new fluffy socks and sat next to him. One of the strangest presents, given to me by the Traffic Warden's aunt, was a copy of *Men Are from Mars, Women Are from Venus* by John Gray. I had never bought into "self-help" of any kind, partially due to the monstrous titles and partially to a terror I had that one day I would wake up and find life-affirming Post-it notes taped to my mirror, in order to make me feel less alone every time I looked at my solitary reflection.

I started flicking through it. Unsurprisingly, it turned out to be a dull, repetitive read. It was meant to explain how men and women are polar opposites but can live in peace together if they only acknowledge a few apparently universal truths:

Men are like rubber bands. They pull away from intimacy. A woman must give them time alone. She must trust that however far a man pulls back, he will eventually realise that he misses the intimacy, and snap back, becoming more intimate than ever. A man needs to feel he has authority.

A woman, however, is like a wave. She has crests and wells. When she is on her crest, she is at her most loving. When she is in her well, a man must support her, and understand that she has a right to be upset. Funnily enough, a woman enters this well roughly every twenty-eight days. This is about the time that her self-esteem drops.

When a man is pulling away and a woman is in her well, things go wrong.

I read parts of it aloud to the Traffic Warden. "Reasons Men Argue: 1. I feel my authority is threatened. I feel inadequate as a man. 2. I feel that I am not needed. I want to be able to provide for my partner. 3…"

His eyes didn't even flicker from the TV.

"OK, this is a waste of time." I turned the page and started laughing, and read aloud again. "Reasons Women Argue: 1. I feel ignored, like my partner doesn't listen to me at all. Sometimes I feel like I don't exist."

By the time I reached the end of the first sentence, he was laughing with me. I put my face in his neck and squeezed him in so tight, as tight as I could. "If you ever feel like pulling away…" but I didn't finish the sentence.

Later in bed, after he'd checked for spiders, I said, "What are you going to be when you grow up?"

"A cunt." He got into bed and folded the pillow so our noses were inches apart.

"Be serious."

"I don't know."

"What, you've got no idea?"

"Yeah. Why does everyone have to have *ambitions* and know where they're going and what suit they're going to buy—"

"Just because you've got an ambition it doesn't make you a city boy."

"No, but everyone *wants* something. Can't they just be content?"

"I don't know if contentment is a true human trait." I closed my eyes.

"I don't want to wear a fucking grey suit."

"I know."

I wanted him to say something, but I wasn't sure what. I kissed him, and started lightly scraping my nails along his inner thigh. I felt him shift and moan softly, and I let him pull me towards him.

*

When I went back to work after Christmas the office seemed slightly darker, as if someone had gone round and changed the bulbs to a lower wattage.

Like Ian, I now had my own mug, as I'd taken in the one that the Traffic Warden's mum had bought me for Christmas.

At three o'clock, I made a cup of tea in it and put it on the submission desk. Young Nathan picked up a similar mug, full of his pens, and pointed at it. His was *Brave New World*.

"That's a good one. Have you read it?"

He looked back at his mug and frowned. "Yeah. It took me about... ten seconds."

"The book."

"No."

"It's good." I took a submission sheet from the tray.

"I don't really read modern books."

"Oh. What do you read?"

"At the moment I'm reading *Nana*." He pulled it out of the top drawer of his desk, and I took it off him and flicked through thin pages of dense prose.

"I used to work with someone called Nana at Macs. A man."

"Interesting. Do you think the book's about him?"

"Shut up. What else do you read?"

"Dostoyevsky."

"Serious?"

"Yeah. Why?"

"I didn't think anyone actually read that stuff." I felt mischievous. "Waste of time to read books written before 1900. Why ride a Wright brothers' plane when you can fly Concorde?"

Young Nathan grimaced. "Are *you* serious?"

"Um... half-serious, yes."

"But you were an *English* student."

"Yeah."

"Did you even pass?"

"Yes, thanks."

"What did you get? 2:1?"

"Something like that." I had got a first, for what good it did me. I started writing the submission numbers down in a little column.

"Me too. And you think *Harry Potter* is better than *Crime and Punishment*?"

"Well, I haven't read either of them, but I'm not talking about *all* modern literature."

"You admit that some modern literature is better than the rest, then?"

"Yeah, of course."

"So the goodness is intrinsic to the work. It doesn't matter when it's written. Any literature can be good."

"It can, it can, it's just—"

He cut me off. "And your analogy about planes doesn't work. Flying in a plane is about getting from A to B, so it's obvious that a Concorde is faster and more efficient and so on, but reading a book is so much more than just getting to a destination."

"Is it?"

"Stop talking bollocks."

I laughed, rubbing my head. "Okay, okay, the analogy is bad. But I do think that sometimes it's very easy to forget that language is... evolving. Every word is like an animal and it's the survival of the fittest: new words get used and old ones become archaic and die out. So why should something that was written over a century ago be held on a pedestal without any questions asked? Yeah, it's wrong to say that all old books are crap, but why accept that I *must* read certain books, because they are *great*, as if they'll do something *good* for me, as if I've got to *gain* something that I didn't have before? If a book's not about getting from A to B, that is."

"That's totally different from what you were saying."

"Maybe."

"So you're changing your argument."

"Maybe."

"Well, even going with your new theory, it's not a waste of time to at least *investigate* old books. I mean, if you were a scientist studying the evolution of man, you'd look back at all the creatures before us as we are now, as they can tell us all about where we've come from, and how and why we are the way we are."

"Yes, but... if you were a doctor treating a human in the present day, you'd just look at the most recent studies, wouldn't you?"

"That's a different question."

I shrugged. "Well, maybe not *that* different."

Young Nathan shook his head. "Let's agree to disagree."

"Okay. Is it just me or are you a bit narked about something?"

"No, not really."

I clicked a few boxes and watched the submission go.

"Well, a bit. My stories keep getting rejected from magazines. I don't know what's wrong with them."

"Let me read one and I'll tell you."

He smiled, but neither of us said anything for a minute.

"You were my Secret Santa, weren't you?"

He smiled again. "Of course."

Before Christmas a fairly high number of agreements had been coming in each day, but it was nothing in comparison to the stacks that came in January.

"Looks like you're going to need a helper," Ian said, taking a sip of coffee.

"Are you volunteering?"

He grimaced. "No."

*

"Tell me something I don't know about you." I was cooking, and the Traffic Warden was on the Xbox. I didn't think he would answer, so I was surprised when he called through to the kitchen.

"I pissed in a boy's shoe once."

We both laughed.

"Why the fuck would you do that?"

"I can't remember. Didn't like him much."

"Yeah, I guess not." I was cutting carrots, and I took him a little disc and fed it straight into his mouth like a treat. "Do you think that you know everything about me?"

103

"No."

"What percentage?"

"What do you mean?"

"What percentage of me is still unknown?"

"Sixty?"

"Come on, I think you know me better than that." But even as I said it, I wasn't certain.

"Well, I know that you question everything."

"Yeah, so?"

"It's actually quite annoying sometimes."

"Better than questioning nothing."

*

About a week later I was entering an agreement when my phone rang. Big Nathan.

I played dumb again and gave my patter as usual.

"Hello."

"Hello."

"Can you come over?"

"Of course."

I went, and stood before his desk as if I was his efficient little secretary.

"Have a look at this." He slid a piece of paper towards me and sat back in his chair.

It was the same job description that I'd replied to in the paper, however many months ago. Too many months.

I noticed an unnecessary apostrophe, but I didn't mention it as I passed it back.

He said, "Well, is it an accurate description of your job?"

It wasn't quite, but I couldn't tell what angle he was coming from, so I said, "More or less."

"Good. Because that's going in the paper on Thursday. I've decided to hire another person to input agreements."

"Oh, right." I smiled. "Is that it?"

"Yes. Thanks."

I went back to my desk.

Rachel was on the phone but raised an eyebrow at me and I checked Big Nathan wasn't looking before miming a yawn.

That evening, Henri Lloyd was staring open-mouthed at Londis as usual, like it was some sight he'd travelled miles to see. Reading Woman sat next to me in the station and I very nearly asked her if she'd had a good Christmas, only just stopping myself.

I hadn't seen Helmet Man since going back to work. Perhaps he'd killed himself. Perhaps he'd taken a long look at his son and young wife and beige carpet and IKEA furniture and hung himself with a string of Christmas fairy lights.

I found a tatty *Metro* and read about how an Argentine man had made a galleon out of a record number of matchsticks. It had taken him seven and a half years and from the pictures I could see he'd reproduced each part with autistic accuracy.

There was a picture of him and his wife, a dour face with flat greasy hair. If I'd been married to him, I'd have waited until the varnish was just dry before taking a sledgehammer to it.

There was nothing else interesting and it was getting too cold to read so I sat in my usual spot, trying not to shiver. I watched a guy in a fluorescent jacket emerge from his hut on the platform with a paddle that was black on one side and white on the other, and I thought that it must be strange to spend your whole day effectively waiting for trains.

I wondered if he was working on a novel at home like Young Nathan, and if it was about fixed destinies and final destinations, as he watched trains clicking along their tracks all day.

*

We were going swimming one evening and walking past the doors of the bottom flats when I heard a moaning sound.

One of the doors was ajar, and I knew it was the old woman's flat because it had a black box outside with a security pad so the nurses could let themselves in without keys.

I turned to the Traffic Warden.

"Do you think we should—" I whispered, because the hallway was so prone to echoing.

"No, come on."

I tried to peer down the gap where her door was open, but all I could see was her hall carpet, which was the colour of digestives. "But she's old, and—"

"I'm not going with you." He kept walking.

I looked back at the door, but I didn't go.

As we were driving through the courtyard I saw Mike, taping a notice onto one of the wheelie bins. I waved but he just turned around and wobbled off.

He always walked like he'd shat himself.

I swam on my back in the slow lane again, alongside the pairs of women who refused to get their hair wet and talked all the way. I'd already predicted, and then heard, the Traffic Warden's thoughts on that, even though he only went in the fast lane.

The gym had free scales in the lobby and when we came out, dripping wet and clammy from the changing rooms, I stood on them. I couldn't remember the last time I'd checked my weight, but was pretty sure I'd gained about a stone in the last three months.

106

In the car I put my hand over my stomach and felt the new roundness. I could grab a handful of it.

"Do you think I'm getting fat?"

The Traffic Warden was drinking out of a bottle of water and nearly spat a mouthful of it into the windscreen. "Since when have you cared about that?"

"I don't, really. It's just, you know, I used to be on the go all the time, and now I sit in an office all day…"

"It's a sign of contentment."

"But I'm not contented."

"How do you mean?"

"I mean I don't want to work in a shitty office or live in a mouldy flat for the rest of my life." I put my hand on his thigh. "I want… something else. I'm not sure what exactly, and I know that's no good because it's not enough to know only what you *don't* want, but I need *something*. Do you know what I mean?"

When we'd been at uni he'd had an incredible knack of knowing what I wanted, even before I did. He'd just read my face and take me to Asda or to the amusements at the seaside, and it seemed to make everything better.

Now, he gave me a long sideways glance.

I sighed. "Look, I know what you're thinking, and you're wrong, okay? I'm not saying I want to go and get some generic high-flying city job, but I *can't* spend the rest of my life picking up the phone and saying the same thing over and over again. Honestly, I think I'm going out of my mind with boredom."

After a long pause I said, "You don't want to be a traffic warden forever, do you?"

He didn't answer but said quietly, "I thought you were getting out of the office."

"I know. I am. I keep forgetting to buy the job paper."

"The newsagent's right next to the station."

"I know."

*

I always knew what the weather was doing and what it was going to do from listening to Ruth on the phone.

All day she said, "It's going to be the coldest day tomorrow, so they say."

The people on the other end of the line might have found this fascinating, but I started to be able to tell with uncanny accuracy when it was coming as well as her precise intonation.

I wasn't sure if I was being unfair or not, but really I thought anyone who was going to volunteer a piece of meaningless information to fifty people across the country for no apparent reason had to be slightly unhinged.

I looked at the reindeer hanging off the back of her in-tray, and wondered who I was to judge her.

I couldn't have cared less about how cold it was, as long as the sky stayed clear.

Towards the middle of January, Big Nathan started interviewing. He saw seven applicants in total and I had to buzz them up, so I got a good look at each one.

There were meant to be eight but one was a no-show. Of the seven, two were teenage boys. One had his shirt hanging out of his trousers and the other swaggered in with his hair gelled into spikes and a pink stripy tie and black shirt. He had hooked his jacket over his shoulder with his finger and within a second I thought he looked like a twat.

The rest were all female. One was small, brown hair, pretty. The other four were nondescript and secretarial.

Rachel and I gawped at each of them as they were led into the office and to the submission computer in order to do the same typing test that I had sat.

I remembered it well.

When I went over at three, I said to Mary, "I wonder if my typing has improved since I last did that test."

"Try it and see."

She set it up for me, and I did.

Young Nathan watched me. "You're gonna mess up in a minute."

"You're gonna get your face smacked in a minute."

As I picked my way through the string of numbers and punctuation I felt sorry for the applicants, as if I had never been one of them.

I sat back when I was done.

"Well?" Mary said.

"I'm worse."

All three of us laughed.

Later I was at the pigeonholes when Big Nathan went over to the kitchen to make himself a cup of tea. It was the first time I'd ever seen him do that.

He called over to me. "Well? What did you think of them?"

"Who?"

"The applicants."

"Oh. Don't know, really. All right. Didn't think much of the one with his shirt hanging out, though."

Big Nathan raised his eyebrows. "He was actually very nice."

"I'm sure he was, but I wouldn't hire anyone who can't tuck their shirt in for an interview."

Ian stifled a laugh.

I nearly added something about the boy in the pink tie, but was glad I didn't because when I went round to put some letters in the pouch for the postman, he was still sitting behind the brown screen, tapping his feet on the carpet, waiting for his interview.

I finished the post and went back to my desk, and watched the boy go over to do his typing test.

I whispered to Rachel about the way he'd walked in with his jacket over his shoulder like a catalogue model. She didn't take her eyes off him.

"He'll get the job."

I glanced back at him. He had very pale skin, a thin face with a bony chin and a spattering of freckles across his nose. He was only young, sixteen or seventeen at the very most, but he looked like a boy racer in the making. "Nah. You reckon?"

"He will. Trust me. I have a feeling about it."

I didn't want to think about it.

Whoever was picked, I was already dreading the humiliating introduction ritual of taking them round the office on their first day in that roll call of forgettable names. I knew already that each person would skew their greeting a little so it didn't sound exactly like the last, the way people tried to think of an original comment to write in a card, but it all ended up sounding exactly the same, and the predictability made it worse than anything else.

Then I'd have to sit down with them and explain what an agreement was and how to input it. Just like Mel had sat down with me.

Little Boy

One dull Wednesday after work, I went to Sainsbury's to get stuff for dinner. Two cans of chopped tomatoes, two balls of mozzarella, and a packet of lasagne sheets. As they were beeped through the checkout I reflected that I would probably never finish a box of sheets and a lasagne at the same time, so I'd have an open box in the cupboard from now until I died. Or maybe it'd be like a solar eclipse and happen once every so many years.

I arrived on the platform only twelve minutes later than usual, though I would still make the 17.24. I saw Helmet Man.

So he hadn't killed himself.

I was strangely warmed.

My bench was full, so I kept going down the platform until I was the furthest away from anyone.

A wind started to blow and I enjoyed the feel of it in my hair after being stifled in the airless office all day.

I propped my bag against my feet and took out my magazine.

At 2.45am on 6 August 1945, Tibbets and his 12-man crew took off from the air base on Tinian Island and headed for the Japanese mainland. No opposition was encountered, and the 8,000lb bomb, code-named "Little Boy", was dropped at 8.15am. The explosion detonated 1,900ft above the city of Hiroshima, killing 20,000 people instantly. Shock and horror swept over the crew. Only Tibbets and US navy captain William "Deke" Parsons had been privy to the full scale of their mission. "Fellows," Tibbets said, "you have just dropped the first atom bomb in history."

Just as I got to the bottom of the article, the train whooshed in behind my magazine. *No opposition was encountered.* I slid the magazine back in my bag, and stepped on the train.

A song came onto my iPod that I could never switch off halfway through. It was my most-listened-to song out of around 3,000, as I had heard it exactly 360 times. The next song down I had only played 267. I loved the play counts in iTunes, though I didn't know why. It wasn't as if I liked the thought of counting anything else, like the number of times I had caught the train to do the same journey, back and forth.

That would depress me beyond belief.

When I got home from work, the Traffic Warden opened the door just as I raised my key to the lock. I had suspected he might do as much, since he was on earlies and got home an hour before me. He always looked curiously pleased with himself each time he foxed me and I stood there with my key pointed like a gun into thin air.

He was still in his uniform, big and dark. I pulled his shirt up and kissed his hairy chest and let it drop back down. He smiled and shut the door. We talked about our days, and how mutually uninteresting they had been.

As I unpacked the shopping I told him about Little Boy.

He shrugged. "So?"

"Well, don't you think it's kind of horrific?"

"Well, not really. They had to do it. Circumstances of war."

"Tell that to all the people he *vaporised*. And his crew, ignorant the whole time. Listen to this: *'I'm not proud that I killed 80,000*

112

people, but I'm proud I was able to start with nothing, plan it and have it work as perfectly as it did,' he said. 'I sleep clearly every night.'"

The Traffic Warden shrugged again. "The guy was just doing his job."

I wanted to say *so were the Nazis* but I knew that people had a go at him all day long for being a traffic warden, so I didn't.

"How many tickets did you give out today?"

He yawned. "Five."

"You know, you really need to sort your clothes out," I told him, when we got into bed. I plucked at his polo shirt, which must once have been bright red but had faded to a brown, like an old scab. It was thin as paper.

"What? I love this shirt—"

"It's horrific. It's an *abomination*."

He laughed at me, and so did I.

"It really is disgusting," I said. "I mean, I know you've got this thing about fashion, and don't worry, nobody thinks you're cool, but there are some standards of decency—"

"Look at yourself! You're wearing my shirt."

"Yeah, it's comfy."

"Yeah, I *know* it is. So's this, anyway."

"At least my clothes are clean."

"What do you mean, *your* clothes?"

I shrugged. "What's yours is mine. You can wear my clothes if you like."

"Don't be a bint."

*

A few days later, Rachel turned to me in the office. "All right, what is it?"

I stopped typing. "What's what?"

"You look excited about something."

I bit my lip and whispered, "Yeah, I am kind of."

She leaned forward. "Did he pop the question?"

"No." I wrinkled my nose. "I have an interview. For the library job."

She did a zip motion over her mouth, but later she came to see me when I was doing the post.

"What are you going to wear?"

"I dunno. Office gear, I guess. What do you think?"

"Power suit."

"Really? I don't own a power suit."

"Invest in one."

I laughed. "Come on, what librarian wears a power suit?"

"You could be the first."

"I don't think so."

"What did you tell Big Nathan?"

"Doctor's appointment."

"Sneaky."

I shrugged and went back to the post. I must've still been smiling, because I could feel her eyes on me.

"I'll miss you if you go."

"I know. I'll miss you too."

"Like fucking hell you will."

*

The following Sunday afternoon I made a roast and we watched *Deal or No Deal*.

At the start of the show, the contestant was certain that her box contained the £250,000 as she got "a feeling" from it.

"Fat *and* deluded," the Traffic Warden said.

114

The round after she eliminated the £250,000, she dealt on fifteen thousand.

"Silly cow."

"I'd've dealt on that," I said.

"You should always go to the end."

I speared a roast potato. "Fifteen grand is a lot of money."

"Yeah, but you only get one chance to go on the show, so you might as well make the most of it. You've got to gamble, that's the whole idea."

"You haven't *got* to. By the very nature of a gamble. And sometimes it's wise to… hedge your bets."

"Rubbish."

"It's not. If I was sitting at home with fifteen grand, I wouldn't really care that it could have been something else. If I'd turned it down and went home with a tenner, I'd be *gutted*."

Even after the contestant dealt, they continued the game to show what would have happened if they'd carried on. We watched as she eliminated three more low numbers, improving the offer to £25,000.

"Are you sure about that?" The Traffic Warden looked almost unbearably smug as he ripped a Yorkshire pudding apart.

"Isn't it weird how they play out the rest of the show, as if she hasn't dealt? I mean, it's boring for us, but what a great thing for the contestant."

The Traffic Warden belched.

"I mean, they can know for sure whether the decision they've made to deal is right or wrong," I said. "It'd be kind of cool if there was an equivalent for life, don't you think?"

"What?"

"Well, what if you could see all the alternate paths, and know whether you'd chosen the right one."

I could see him thinking as he chewed. "I can't think of

anything worse."

"Why?"

"Because some things it's better not to know."

"But your life can only ever be one way. Even though you have choice, or the illusion of choice, there is only ever one outcome. So your box contains a definite number. You can't just deny that and say it doesn't matter —"

"But it *doesn't*." He'd finished his meal and was making a chopping motion with his hand.

"Of course it does! I want to know that things get better than this. I want to know what's worth trying for and what's a waste of time. I want to know what job I'm going to end up doing, where we end up living. I want to know *everything* about my life."

"Now you're just being silly." The Traffic Warden wiped his finger through his gravy and licked it.

"I'm not. Imagine all your potential is in a marked box. Aren't you desperate to open it?"

"Maybe – but the game's not really about what's in the box, is it?"

I had just got to the best part of the roast, the meat, which I always saved for last. "The interview for that library job is this week."

"When?"

"Tuesday afternoon. It sounds so good. I really hope I get it."

"Well, don't get your hopes up too high. You don't want to be disappointed."

"Thanks."

*

I was fifteen minutes early for the interview, and not sure who to ask when I got there. As all the librarians at the desk were dealing with people, I asked a woman in a cerise jumper who was stacking books onto trolleys, and as she turned I could see that her hair was yellow-orange, the colour of fire, and so curly it stuck out on end.

She looked very put out by my enquiry. "You'll have to see them at the desk about that."

"They look very busy over there."

"Well, yes, we all are, aren't we?"

"Sorry."

"Oh, well, never mind, I'll take you, I'll take you."

I wondered why she was so bothered about me asking her if she was going to help me anyway.

"Wait here," she said, pointing to a chair next to a block of computers.

"Okay." I sat down and watched her disappear through a door.

I tried to look professional, but it was difficult as I was sitting with the people waiting to use the computers and they kept looking at me bizarrely as I let them skip me.

After ten minutes passed, I started to wonder about the intentions of the cerise curly woman, and asked one of the women behind the desk.

She looked at me as if I was the mad one. "Right, okay." She came out from behind the desk and I followed her short grey hair and pastel blouse back across the library, past the computers and through a battered door marked *Staff Only*.

I waited in a room that was entirely lined with those grey tin filing cabinets, even though it wasn't big enough at all. From my knowledge of filing and filing cabinets I could see that if they were all open simultaneously there would just be enough space in the middle of the room for two chairs.

I became almost desperate to know what was inside them and I really wanted to open one and flick through the contents, but I just sat with my hands folded in my lap, until eventually the door opened.

A woman entered and I got up straight away, as if I was guilty of something. She was tall and had grey, shoulder-length hair and a grey power suit with a white, ribbed turtleneck underneath. I smiled and shook her hand.

Then I saw that behind her, there was another interviewer: Reading Woman, from the train.

*

"How was it?" the Traffic Warden asked. He had had a day off and I could tell he'd spent the whole day eating on the sofa and playing on the Xbox.

"Weird." I took off my coat and hung it over the door as our flat had no hooks. "There were two interviewers, and get this: one of them is someone I always see on the train." It didn't sound as interesting as I'd thought it would.

"So?"

"Oh, I don't know, it's just weird. I don't think I'll get the job, though I *really* want it. They had all these boxes to fill in on teamwork and customer service skills, and the main interviewer said *equal ops* about ten times. I'm not kidding. It was pretty sickening."

"Well, they're run by the council, aren't they?"

"It shows. I really wanted to say I was half-African or a fucking lesbian or something. So they could feel like they were representing some sort of oppressed minority." I started towards the kitchen to get some water, as my teeth had started aching again. "You'd think they'd get tired of ticking boxes all fucking day. I mean, they're human, you know, they *know* that not everything can be quantified on paper, but we can't acknowledge that, so we all have to sit and participate in a complete *sham*."

"You should infiltrate the system, and bring it down from the inside."

It was what I used to say when I worked at Macs. "Yes, yes, very funny." I took two Anadin.

"Actually, perhaps you should go and work back at McDonald's for a bit. The one down the road's hiring."

I pulled my shirt off over my head and threw it at him. "Don't be a cunt all your life."

*

That night, I dreamt I was walking around an indoor market in a huge tent. On the trestle tables were not antiques or clothes, but female heads, upright with their necks totally flat on the surface, like bronze wig mannequins.

They were hairless, with closed eyes and silent mouths. The first one I saw was plain, but all the others had been made up with metallic turquoise or purple eyeshadow swept across their lids. They were all strikingly beautiful, with elongated eyes and high cheekbones.

I walked amongst them, an unseen observer, until I came to one that was not just a head, but the whole of the body above her hips.

I went over, slowly. Her arms were moving, so I thought she was alive and I realised that all the heads might be too. I looked under the table, but there was nothing there to explain it. There was no blood, and no sign of butchery.

"Is it a trick?" I asked.

She became animated, rocking back and forth, laughing and talking manically. She was like one of those old fortune-teller machines in fairgrounds where a robot in a turban is sitting in a box. I was aware, though, that somewhere beneath her mechanical exterior she was human, and even though I knew I wasn't going to get through, I didn't want to give up.

I touched her body, where it met the table. "Did it hurt?"

But she just kept talking and rocking, and I kept asking, "Did it hurt? Did it hurt?"

And then I woke up.

*

As I stepped out of the office one night, I fell into exact step with a man going down the road.

It jarred me to be so in sync with a stranger, and I slowed my pace and followed his sharp steps all the way to the station.

He had a carrier bag in his hand, which I could see contained a book, and I watched his arm move forwards and backwards pendulum-like, towards me and away from me, the loose plastic flapping in the dark wind, everything around us lit by the orange streetlights.

When we got to the station, I watched him sit down on my bench, fold his legs neatly and take his book out.

He pushed his glasses up his nose and stroked his fingers gently through his short beard. He looked intelligent. More than intelligent. He looked kind and logical, destined to be a professor some day. I stood behind him, staring at the pale curve of his neck where it rose out of his corduroy jacket. I wondered if I could ever have ended up with someone like him.

I imagined a conversation we might have and he'd say, *What, you don't know such and such?* and I'd be forced to admit that I really knew nothing about history, geography, or politics. He would look at me with pity and only ever see me as deficient, whereas the Traffic Warden saw my vast areas of complete ignorance as an eccentricity on my part.

Sometimes I got the impression the Traffic Warden thought I was some sort of genius and even though I knew I was far from it, I tried not to do or say anything that would stop him thinking it. I was no better than those women who did their make-up before their husband woke up.

Or perhaps that's all love really is: recognising someone's flaws but not really seeing them as faults at all.

Once I had gone out with someone who said I was *too passionate about all the wrong things*. I had smiled and nodded and told him he was probably right, even though I knew there were no right things and even if there were, choice never came into it.

You love what you love and you believe what you believe.

The Traffic Warden would never say anything like that to me, and for a second I ached for him to be standing beside me.

Then the 17.24 came, as all trains do, with a smooth rush of air and a long squeak, distant like a dog whistle.

*

When I got back, the Traffic Warden was rifling through the drawers on the coffee table, his hand against his head.

"Hello," I said, picking up the post. "Everything okay?" I flicked through the envelopes, and there was one from the council. The envelope was thin, far too thin for a contract.

"Yeah, life's a fucking bowl of cherries." I could hear a bass line through the ceiling. He slammed the drawer shut. "Those fucking *cunts* have decided to have a fucking *disco* upstairs. Have you seen my cigarettes?"

"No." I ripped open the letter. *We are sorry to inform you ... We wish you every success in the future.* I put it on the bed and opened the second letter. It was another questionnaire from my old university. *Please contact us...* I left it on the bed and pulled my shirt over my head in the lounge doorway. "Yeah, my day was good, thanks for asking."

"Have you got a lighter?"

"For God's sake, I gave you one yesterday. Are you a Bermuda Triangle for—"

"Look, have you got one or not?"

"Don't snap at me just because you're in a bad mood."

He sat heavily in the deckchair. "Oh, shut up."

"Fuck you." I stormed to the bedroom and slammed the door with all my might, like a teenager.

Maybe five minutes passed.

The door opened, and he came and sat beside me and hugged me.

"I'm sorry."

"It's all right."

"I'm just an arsehole, you know that."

"You're not an arsehole." I ran my finger round the curve of his ear. "I know the neighbours get on your nerves, but you have to find some way to deal with it that doesn't involve us yelling at each other."

"Mike'll be up next."

"Exactly. And we don't want that."

We both made a noise somewhere between a laugh and a sniff.

"Do you think we can live somewhere really remote?" he asked. "You know, North Scotland or something?"

I leaned my head against his chest. "It rains in Scotland. A lot."

"I like rain."

"I don't. Remote sounds good, though."

We paused.

"I didn't get that library job."

"I'm sorry." He kissed my hair and started to stroke my thigh, and I remembered that all I had on was underwear. "You know you have very, very soft legs…"

I kissed him on the mouth and he kissed me back.

He lay back on the bed and I climbed on top of him and pinned him to the sheets. He still had his work shirt on, epaulettes and all. I imagined that he was a pilot. He made to get out of my grip but I held fast and whispered, "You're not allowed to touch me."

I nuzzled his neck and went for his lips but as soon as he kissed me back I pulled away. I felt him shifting beneath me like sand and I stretched back, pressing my breasts into him. I liked the feel of his tummy hair on them, furry and warm. "I've got you pinned, and you can't get out of it."

Afterwards I said, "I can't believe I had you pinned."

He was stroking my hair. "You didn't."

I propped myself on an elbow. "I did too."

"Okay, pin me again."

"You just want an excuse to make me climb on top of you again."

He shrugged. "You can't do it."

I held his wrists against the pillow, as hard as I could, and he sat up with barely a fight, picked me up and spun me around until I was flat on my back and dizzy and unable to speak from giggling.

We lay there for a minute, listening to the bass from upstairs, although the Traffic Warden didn't say anything. I got up and so did he, and we both looked out the window, as if to check the world was still there.

Mini Man was smoking on the wall outside with his girlfriend.

"Why is Mini Man's girlfriend always so moody?" the Traffic Warden asked.

"I dunno. Maybe that's just her natural expression. I think I have a bit of a moody face."

"You don't."

"Hope not." I pulled a baggy T-shirt over my head. "What do you want for dinner?"

"What have we got?"

"Nothing."

"Do you want to go shopping?"

"Not really."

"Come on, moody bum."

I smiled. "Oh, yeah, *I'm* the moody one..."

When we got there someone was putting the yellow stickers on the bakery stuff. *Reduced Reduced Reduced* coming out of a tape gun and people swarming round. We wanted some naan bread but couldn't get anywhere near the shelves, so we stood there waiting while people picked through packets, turning over products in their hands and scrutinising them as if they needed vital information about bread.

"Fuck this," the Traffic Warden said, then he shouted, "Quick, everyone, come on, stock up, the apocalypse is coming!"

No one even looked up.

The Traffic Warden wandered off at some point between Bread and Canned Vegetables, so I was left alone, pushing the trolley. I put in some sweetcorn and a couple of tins of chopped tomatoes and was just wondering how chopped tomatoes could be more tomatoey than real tomatoes, when I saw a tin of Value Meatballs and put them in too.

I knew that they'd be disgusting, that I'd open them up one day when in desperate need of a warm snack and they'd smell like cat food and the sauce would be thin and taste of metal, and the balls themselves would be pale and pinkish inside.

I also knew that they'd remind me of sitting in our dirty student kitchen watching the lunchtime edition of *Neighbours*, spooning them in with little chunks of half-melted cheese.

The Traffic Warden didn't see them until we were standing next to the conveyor belt. "Meatballs? Mmm, they look nice."

I took them from his hand and put them back next to the jar of pickled onions.

Shaun

On the way to work one morning I read in the *Metro* that researchers in Tokyo had developed a robot that could play the violin, and for about a week I watched the online video of it almost obsessively. It was quite spooky to hear the mournful tune played with no passion whatsoever.

I was putting my lunch in the fridge when Mary twisted round in her chair and said, "Kim's had her baby."

I'd known it was coming, but I was still sort of surprised. Since we all already knew that it was a girl, I wasn't sure what to ask.

"How is she?"

"She's doing just fine."

"That's good. Has she named her?"

"Yeah. Lexi, Laxi, something like that."

"Right."

When I went back to my desk I told Rachel.

She smiled. "Now the hard work starts."

"How d'you mean?"

"I mean, if she thinks the pregnancy was bad, it'll be nothing in comparison to this. She'll be back. You wait."

My phone rang. It was Big Nathan and I said my usual prattle.

"Hello, it's me. Just to let you know, we have a new data inputter starting today – he's coming about half nine, if you could show him the ropes?"

"Him?"

"Yes. Don't worry, I didn't pick the one with his shirt hanging out."

No, he'd picked the boy racer.

"Okay," I said. "No worries."

After I put the phone down I wanted to smash my face into the desk, but restrained myself since Big Nathan was right across the office.

"What's up?" Rachel asked.

"You were right, you cow."

She winked. "Always am."

Thankfully, he didn't walk in with his jacket over his shoulder this time, but he had spiked and gelled his hair again, and had the same stripy shirt and tie combination.

"Hi," I said. "Sorry, I haven't been told your name…"

He sniffed and wiped his hand across his nose and nodded all at once, but didn't help me out.

"And your name is?"

"Shaun." He grinned and his eyes darted around the office, as if he was about to shoplift something. He didn't ask me who I was.

"Right." I took a deep breath. "Well, I'll take you round the office, then."

As the only free computer was the one opposite Young Nathan, I had to sit Shaun there, which wasn't particularly convenient for training as I had to keep going to get things from my desk.

I asked Mary to take the reception phone for a bit and I dragged my chair over to him. "Right. Well, this is an agreement. And I'm going to show you how to input it."

I explained to him about the three different systems: MRP, ICS, and CRS. Then I showed him how to log onto the MRP system, the easiest one to start with.

He kept looking around the office and constantly jigged and jittered in his chair, so I was relieved after I'd gone through the basics to offload some easy batches onto him and go back to my desk to get on with my own work.

"Is he on speed or something?" Rachel whispered.

"I dunno, but I think Big Nathan was when he hired him."

The morning was quiet, and I was disappointed. Shaun asked me no questions and this was not a good sign: it meant either he wasn't doing any work or he wasn't picking out anomalies in the agreements, of which there must have been some.

I asked Big Nathan if he minded me going on lunch at normal time while I was training Shaun, and he said it was okay.

Rachel was pleased and so was I. We ate our sandwiches together at our desks and then went outside for a fag.

She sat down on a low wall, which trimmed an island of plants, including low purple clouds that looked a bit like heather. I noticed the first bumblebees of spring fussing round them, and stepped away. Rachel got up too.

"I like bees," I said.

"Not that close."

One flew near me and I leaned away. "No."

"They're telepathic, you know."

I laughed. "Shut up."

"No, seriously, they are. My great-aunt's a leading authority on bees and that's what she said."

I was still laughing. "Rachel, come on, how can that be? Even if it was true, how would we be able to verify it?"

A bee flew past again, and landed on the purple flowers. I leaned in towards it slightly. "Hello, Mr Bumblebee. Hey, quick, think of a number and I'll ask him what it is."

She was smiling now too. "Well, my aunt believes it, and that's enough for me."

"So if I said I believed in God, would that be enough for you to believe it?"

"I do."

"Really?"

"Yeah."

"So do you believe in the afterlife?"

"Yeah. Sort of. I think that life is circular, so our souls never die."

I lit a second fag off the first and so did she. "Well, how do you explain population growth?"

"There's a waiting room."

"But how did they get in there?" I felt as if I was about five, asking my mum where babies came from.

She flicked her fringe out of her eyes and shrugged slightly. "God."

I nodded.

"I think atheists are very sad," she said.

I wasn't offended, though maybe I should have been. "Really?"

"Yeah."

"My parents are staunch atheists," I said. I realised my mistake as soon as the words were out. "I kind of like to be open," I carried on. But I knew it was useless. She didn't say anything else.

I did the default letters in the afternoon to help Ruth out, and they were so boring I felt like I was drifting in and out of consciousness. I kept imagining souls like jellyfish, all fbaty and iridescent, sitting on chairs as if they were waiting for the dentist.

All I could hear was Shaun talking to Young Nathan. His voice was a pitch above the rest of the usual office noises of typing, the swishing of the photocopier, the printer, people saying the same things over and over into the phone.

Every time I looked at him he was doing no work. He thought I was stupid and hadn't noticed anything.

At about four, Big Nathan's daughter came in to do the shredding, which was stacked up at the back in big plastic boxes. Most of it was the returned post from debt collection, or old contracts from customer services. I had a five-ream paper box under my desk for my shredding – most of that was archived records, or the very occasional accidental print-out – so I'd only had to empty it twice.

I loved the shredder.

As the agreements were legal documents they were sacrosanct, but every so often, I came across one that had been sent to us by mistake and didn't need inputting. It gave me incredible pleasure to post it into the slit-mouth of the shredder when nobody was looking, and watch something that should have been precious get sucked in and be destroyed.

*

"You know the old woman in the downstairs flat?"

"Yeah."

"I think she's carked it."

The Traffic Warden was in his uniform and bare feet, eating bread out of the bag and looking out the window.

I'd just hand-washed a jumper that I'd got for Christmas and was trying to think of a way to dry it without wringing. I laid out a towel on the bed so I could roll it up inside and squeeze the water out. "You're such a net curtain twitcher."

"There's a moving van out there."

The radio was on in the kitchen, so the conversation filtered through to the bedroom. They were having a phone-in about engagements and marriage, and we listened to a caller tell the story of meeting his other half online, and then getting married within two weeks of meeting.

The flat seemed suddenly full of this man's voice, and I started to feel like his words were coming from the ether. "I don't know…" the bloke was saying, "I don't know why you'd want to wait. If you know you love someone, and you want to be with them and you can commit to them, then why wait?"

"What are *you* waiting for?" I asked.

He turned to me suddenly and said, "I'm not waiting for anything."

And for an instant I thought he was going to ask me to marry him right there, as I stood in my joggers with unwashed hair, pressing the towel roll onto the bed as if I were suffocating someone with a pillow.

I could feel my own heartbeat.

"I'm not waiting. I'm just being nosy. I'm trying to think… they *must* be moving into the old woman's flat, there's no one else it can be. I mean, Mike's not dead. Yet. But there was no *To Let* sign." He turned back to the window. "Oh, and here comes the Merc…"

I unrolled the towel. It was soaked through, a dark jumper-shaped water patch.

"And look at the state of *that*… She's got one of those yippy little dogs. Eurgh. Oh my God, come and have a look, she's got a bright pink lead. Hey, I might go out there and sniff round her car in my uniform, pretend I'm on duty."

I started rooting in the wardrobe for a strong hanger. "And you wonder why people hate traffic wardens."

*

131

According to Ruth, "The weather just can't make up its mind!"

She said it all day into the phone until I felt like driving a staple into my own forehead. She was right, though: there was the first hint of something humid in the air, something almost sticky.

I didn't like it.

I spoke to a guy who needed customer services but just wouldn't hold. He'd decided that because he was talking to a real person he was going to start a debate, but the truth was that his only options were holding or hanging up.

"Look, darling, I know what it's like," he said. "I work in a call centre too."

"This isn't a call centre," I replied. "It's a small office. I don't have any lines free. If it's longer than a few minutes, I'll come back to you, okay?"

"I'm on a mobile."

My phone chirped, which meant another call was trying to get through.

"Well, I can pass a number on for you," I said.

"Are they going to call me back?"

"I can't guarantee it, but I promise you I'll pass it on."

He started to dictate his number and I wrote it on a yellow note.

"That's only ten digits," I said. My phone chirped again, so there were now two calls waiting.

He repeated it and there was meant to be a nine between the last two digits.

"Okay, I'll pass that on."

He asked me to read it back to him and as I did it the phone chirped again.

"Is anyone actually going to ring me back?"

"Yes, as soon as they have a chance."

"Well, be sure that they do, all right, sweetheart?"

Right then, a huge gust of wind blew all the blinds inwards. Rachel, Kyle and Jackie were all on the phone too, and so none of us could immediately get up; instead we hunkered down as if ducking a low-flying plane.

The bloke hung up and my phone started ringing straight away for the other calls, but the wind was still blowing, and papers in people's letter trays started violently flapping. Even Rachel was caught off-guard, and stumbled over her words.

Ruth's *Sensible Shoes* mug went over and her pens scattered across her desk.

I thought the apocalypse had come at last.

But then the wind stopped as quickly as it had started. I leaned back in my chair and looked out of the window. The air had turned grey and heavy and the sky had formed a thick covering of opaque clouds.

The AquAid man, with his navy uniform and clipboard, was unloading blue plastic tanks of water.

I was still holding the bloke's yellow note. *Be sure that they do, sweetheart.* I looked at it for a long time before flicking it into the bin.

*

"Are you coming to the gym?"

It was a Saturday and I was reading on the bed. "No. I'm done with the gym."

He put his hand on my stomach and wiggled it. "You'll get a fat bel-ly…"

I flicked him off. "You'll get a black ey-e."

"Suit yourself. But don't come moaning to me when you become morbidly obese."

"Don't come running to me when I stab you in the head with a knife."

He craned suddenly, to look out the window. "Have you seen him?" he asked.

I sat up and looked too. The man across the road seemed to be permanently ripping his front garden to pieces. He had a jumper over his shoulders, knotted at the sleeves on his chest like a medallion. Even though it was winter, his skin was tanned and his shorts were white.

"He looks like a German tennis player," the Traffic Warden said. It was exactly what he looked like.

"Yeah, he does."

When the Traffic Warden got in from the gym, he lay next to me on the bed and put his leg over me. I felt squashed and safe.

"I think that Mercedes belongs to the old woman's daughter, you know."

"Really? That's exciting."

"The black box outside the flat is gone, and that car is there all the time."

"Lucky you didn't go out in your uniform and start sniffing around, then, isn't it?"

"Yeah, I guess so."

I put my book down. "Why *are* you so fascinated by other people's lives?"

"I want a curry," he said.

"All right, then. We'll order at six." That was when India Garden opened.

He spoke to my stomach as if I was pregnant and he was trying to communicate with the baby. "Belly belly belly... belly loves curry."

I laughed. "Fuck off, will you?"

"Belly wants her curry."

"She sure does."

"You're ordering."

He'd done it the last two times, so I couldn't deny it was my turn. "Okay. Thing is, I never get the greeting you do."

"They don't like you as much."

"I know."

It started raining, like claws on the window. He rubbed my side with his thumb and I could feel his erection move on my back.

I tugged his arm hair.

"Ow."

I pulled it again.

"Stop it, will you?"

"No."

"Right—"

And we wrestled until we were breathless.

*

I was making coffee for Rachel and me and trying to pick the least stained teaspoon out of all the ones in the sink when Big Nathan called me over to his desk.

"How's Shaun working out?"

Shaun had messed up three large batches of agreements that morning, so I'd spent most of my day sorting it out. His penance, I'd decided, was to do my filing, so I'd sent him up the back to do it.

Although he wasn't in earshot, I felt a bit caught out. "Er... he's okay. Not the best typist. Needs time to settle in, maybe."

"He was the best typist out of that lot."

"Really?"

I knew he was a good typist; it was just that he talked *all the*

135

time. I had started to feel quite sorry for Young Nathan, who had to listen to it.

"You need to train him," he said.

I was almost offended, as I'd told Shaun far more than I'd ever been told myself. "I'll try," I said.

I thought how peculiar it was that I felt more loyalty towards the boy who made my job harder than I did towards the man who paid me to do it.

"Have you seen *Star Wars*?" Big Nathan asked.

"Yes."

"Well, think of him as Luke Skywalker. And you're Obi-Wan Kenobi." He sat back and smiled, as if he'd made a brilliant connection between my world and his. "So train him. Okay?"

I was almost too surprised to speak. I think I opened my mouth and then closed it again. And then I said, "Yes. Fine."

*

The Traffic Warden and I went to the cinema to watch a two-hour film about oil-drilling.

I went to the toilet before the film started, and on the doors of the cubicles there were gold plastic stars and the names of actresses. I chose Kate Winslet, who was between Whoopi Goldberg and Sharon Stone.

On the inside of the door was a sticker for a domestic abuse help line. Someone had stuck a label over the old address with a new one because too many husbands had tracked their wives to the refuge.

Sometimes, like the time I got my first period when we were on holiday and I couldn't go wading in a river with my brothers, my mum would say, "Who'd be a girl, eh?" and I'd just laugh, as if it was a joke.

When I got back to our seats, the Traffic Warden had bought popcorn, so I reached out to take some.

"Get off. You should have said something sooner. I'd've bought you some if you'd said."

"And I'd of said if you'd asked."

"*Have*, not *of*."

I darted my hand towards the box, and he moved it away, propelling a shower of popcorn onto the red carpet of the aisle. He bent down and threw some at me.

One bounced off my head and we both laughed.

The others stuck to my sweatshirt like those seeds with tiny hooks that stick to dogs' fur, and I picked them off and ate them one by one.

*

"Yes, it's still cloudy here too…"

It was Ruth.

I had become so adept at listening to one side of a telephone conversation that I had started filling in the gaps in my head.

"Mmm… Mmm… Yes, I did wonder about that… Mmm… Well, yes, I mean, actually I did leave here a few years ago, but I came back after a few months. If you find a place that's right and you just stay there, don't you? Yeah… Mmm. Well, I'm glad you're back anyway… Yeah, and you. Okay… nice talking to you, Yasmina. Bye."

Mark

That afternoon Mark the IT guy came over.

He sat next to Big Nathan, just on a slightly smaller desk, like his right-hand man, I assumed by virtue of having programmed one of the databases we used. I'd never seen a single sheet of paper on his desk, only his computer and a selection of sport-themed corporate toys: a little squashy rugby ball, a pad of Post-it notes shaped like a tennis racket, and a real cricket ball in a box.

"Hi," he said, standing awkwardly in his lemon-yellow shirt. He had his hand in his pocket and was jiggling change, which I thought was a strange habit for a man under thirty.

"Hello," I replied, smiling. "Welcome to the dark side."

He frowned. "Er... thanks. Just wanted to let you know, there should be a couple of desks arriving in a bit. I'm going out now and the man needs to be paid in cash, so here it is." He handed me an envelope.

"Okay, no problem."

"So just make sure all the bits are there and give him that envelope."

I nearly joked that I wasn't a drug runner, but resisted. "No problem."

"Good."

After he'd gone out, Rachel turned to me and whispered, "Oh, God, we're going to be split up."

I looked over at Shaun. He was in the kitchen, making his fifth cup of tea.

"If they sit me with Shaun, I'll kill someone," I said. "Either him or myself."

She grinned, but she was a kinder person than me. "He's sweet."

"He *talks*."

"He's young."

"He does less than a *third* of the agreements that I do. And he doesn't answer the phone, or do submission."

"Really?"

"Yep. And it's really started to get on my nerves."

Ruth looked up from her computer. "I have to say I do agree with you. I mean, you two chat but you do get on with your work."

The buzzer went.

The desks.

*

Sunday evening, and I was reading on the bed when the Traffic Warden crawled up the covers towards me so his head was right behind my book.

"*Fat Is a Feminist Issue*," he read out from the cover. "Is that what the belly is? A feminist issue?" He put his hand on my stomach again and wobbled it. It had become a game of his. "Belly loves curry."

I slapped his hand. "Oh, go away, will you?"

"Come on, I'm just kidding around."

"Yes, I'm sure."

"Oh, get a sense of humour."

"Fuck off."

He started to walk out of the room. "Excuse me for trying to have some fun."

I lowered the book and sat up. "Oh, yeah, and what a *noble* ambition that is, thank fuck for *you*."

"What's got into you?"

"Well, I might have more fun if I wasn't doing eighty per cent of the housework, or sitting in interviews getting sized up to see if I plan to get knocked up any time soon. Why don't *you* try being relegated to reception only to be fucking patronised, and changing *your* name when you get married, all the time being made to feel paranoid about your body shape and —"

"You don't do eighty per cent of the housework."

"Oh, really? When was the last time you hoovered? Or bleached the toilet?"

"I wash up."

"Congratu-fucking-lations." I picked the book back up and pretended to carry on reading.

"Well, if it's so shitty living with me, then why don't you just leave?"

"Oh, yeah, you'd love *that*, wouldn't you? Except there'd be no one to cook and no one to *fuck*."

He walked out and slammed the bedroom door.

I threw the book as hard as I could, and it hit the wardrobe and fluttered to the floor like a dead bird. I looked out the window and all I could see was the off-white sky, blank as paper. I missed the cold blue that had been there all winter, but I knew it wasn't going to come back. This was it.

"I'm sorry." I stood in the doorway of the lounge with my arms folded. My face felt stiff with dry tears.

He was in the deckchair, smoking. He didn't turn around. "It's all right."

I went over and stood as he hugged me.

"Do you ever feel like we're playing house?" I asked.

"Not really. Do you?"

A *yeah* would have been truthful but I couldn't bear it, so I said, "Sometimes."

"Why?"

"I don't know."

Neither of us said anything for a long time.

"Is this it, then?"

"Is this what?"

"Nothing."

*

The next day I got to the office at the usual time. I couldn't put my lunch away because Erica was in the kitchen, so I took a pad of Post-it notes, a pen, and my spiral-bound notebook out of my drawer and waited.

There was something missing.

I listened to the office as if it was an orchestra, trying to isolate the sound that wasn't there.

And then I remembered that Mary was on holiday for the week.

My phone started ringing. It was Big Nathan.

"Good morning, you're through to reception, how can I help?"

"I have a job for you."

"Oh. Hello."

"Come over."

"Okay."

I stood in front of his desk. I could hear my phone starting ringing from across the office.

"Can you type?" he asked.

As I was a data input clerk and I'd been there for nearly nine months, I tried hard to think of a sarcastic reply, but I had trouble thinking of something that wasn't offensive.

"I'd hope so," I said.

If he detected my horror he made no outward sign of it. "Well, can I set you a little task?"

"Yes."

"Can you type this letter? I mean, the formatting and things." He held out a piece of paper. As far as I could see, the formatting consisted of knowing how to move text left or right and justifying it, and putting some bullet points in.

"I think I can manage that," I said.

"Okay."

"No problem."

By the time I got back, my phone had stopped ringing and I was glad. Answering it and saying the same thing over and over had started to make me hate my own voice.

All day long people in the office asked me peculiar questions about Mary's job, about envelopes and letterheads and things like that. I couldn't answer anything, and I hoped it wasn't going to stay like that all week.

Mary and I did completely different jobs. It was just that she covered me on the phone when I went for lunch and we collaborated on ordering the stationery. Beyond that and the little jobs that Big Nathan asked her to do, I had no real idea about what her job entailed.

That afternoon, I was on the phone listening to Mrs Shaw catalogue her communications with our office.

I couldn't help her and I'd known that from the start of the phone call, but she seemed like she wanted to talk to someone, anyone, and I didn't have the heart to interrupt.

"So I gave her my reference number, what I thought was my reference number. It was on the letter, dated…"

I watched Rachel attempting to staple something, without much luck. I put Mrs Shaw on mute, so I could hear her but she couldn't hear me. "I'll order you a new stapler if you like," I said to Rachel. "One day I might not be here to fix it for you."

I took Mrs Shaw off mute. "Okay, I think I need to put you through to—"

"Oh, fuck," Rachel said, and a little cascade of bent staples tinkled onto the desk.

Mrs Shaw hadn't finished. "So then I thought, well, you know, I'd had enough. And I phoned your office and couldn't get through, there was an answerphone message and then the line was busy, and—"

I held out my hand to Rachel like a long-suffering mum, and she gave me the stapler. I opened its jaws and peered inside.

"The stapler whisperer," she said, and I struggled not to laugh.

Mrs Shaw continued. "I mean, I get this letter and it just doesn't make any sense, so I got back to the place and they said to ring you…"

I breathed deeply and recovered myself.

"Are you still there, dear?"

"Yes, Mrs Shaw. Do you have your reference number at all?"

"Reference? Let me see, it's here somewhere…"

I heard rustling on the line while she sorted through her papers, and swung round on my chair to get a paperclip from my drawer. I bent it out of shape and used it to release a pair of staples lodged in the teeth. I handed the stapler back to Rachel and held my hand up by my face like a horse's blinker, so I couldn't catch her eye.

Later on, Rachel turned to me and whispered, "God, the atmosphere is so fucking oppressive at the moment, don't you think?"

"It always is."

"It's worse at the moment."

"Mary's not here."

"It's not the same without her."

"No, it's not."

On the way home, I bought the Traffic Warden a little Venus fly trap in a pot from the flower shop outside the station.

I was going to buy him some flowers as a joke, but it was an expensive gag when I knew he'd hate them. I'd never really understood flowers, since all you can do is watch them die.

I got on the same carriage as Reading Woman and I wondered where she'd been because it was the first time I'd seen her since the interview. She didn't look as if she recognised me, but she did purse her lips at the fly trap.

"I don't know if it'll last very long," I said to the Traffic Warden, when I handed it over. "But I... saw it and thought of you."

"Thanks."

We spent the next half-hour picking dead insects out of the lampshade in the lounge with my eyebrow tweezers and tickling the backs of the little green mouths. I was amazed that they really did snap shut – I'd thought it was only something that happened in cartoons, like dogs running with strings of sausages in their mouths.

I started buying exotic fruits on the way home from work.

The first one I bought was purple and slightly bigger than an egg. After dinner one night, I got a knife and a small plate and cut into it lengthways. I imagined that it would be soft inside, with sweet flesh like a plum, only pink. Instead its skin was more like a dry husk, and white inside with the consistency of wet fur. It was filled with black seeds that were covered in some yellow mucus, like tadpoles.

I sucked some up and they made the inside of my mouth contract, like cranberry juice.

"Do you want some?" I asked, holding out a piece.

The Traffic Warden was reading Ceefax. "No. What is it, anyway?"

And even though everything was labelled well enough in the supermarket so I knew it was a passion fruit, I said, "I don't know."

As we got into bed, I said, "I have a bone to pick with you."

He was doing the spider check. "What?"

"We need to discuss the towel situation."

"Do we?"

"Yeah. What is the deal with this peculiar towel habit of yours?"

"What towel habit?"

"This thing you have, the three towels. It seems totally unnecessary. Even if you rotated towels, you'd only need two. But you don't even rotate! You wash them all at the same time. And then we have them drying round the flat forever and a day. I mean, what the hell do you need three towels for?"

"What's it to you?"

"What it is to me is that there's no space in the bathroom for me to hang my towels up. I mean, I have two, one for body and one for hair, but my hair is longer than an inch, so it's necessary. But I can't hang even one of them up in the bathroom. I have to drape one across my bookshelf every morning, and the other over the door, which is dusty. Have you ever noticed that? Have you ever seen me doing that? It's because you inexplicably have three towels. What use can you have for that number?"

"One is for body, one for face and hair, one for arse."

"You've got to be kidding me."

"No. What's wrong with that? I'm trying to be clean."

"Well, it's ludicrous. You're clean when you get out of the shower, so what do you think you're wiping off? It's only water, or a little residual soap."

"That reminds me, can we change the shower gel?"

"Why?"

"That one makes me feel all slippery, like an otter."

"Oh, get whatever fucking shower gel you want. Back to the towel thing—"

"You're nuts."

"—because there's something else: you wash them *all* every few days. You should be able to survive with one towel for at least two weeks – I don't think I even wash my towels once a *month*. The flat's already damp, so the last thing we need is three huge towels drying all the time. Think of the moisture they're putting into the air."

"So? It's not our flat."

"No, but it *is* our deposit, and if we don't take care of the mould we'll get charged."

"That's ridiculous."

"Don't start getting indignant when you haven't cleaned a

single spore of mould from this place."

"We shouldn't be charged."

"Yeah, well, a lot of things shouldn't be, but they are."

"If that cunt thinks he's taking a penny —"

"What? What are you gonna do if he takes a hundred, two hundred pounds?"

"I'll take him to court, until he gives back every fucking penny."

"Don't be silly."

"I will."

"Just sort out the towel situation, will you, please? That's all I'm asking."

I flicked off the light.

*

I wasn't sure if it was the addition of Shaun to the office or Mary's return, but the atmosphere had begun to slightly loosen. I was standing at the photocopier, hand on hip, which seemed to be the only way to stand there, when I noticed that Ian had taken his tie off and coiled it on his desk.

My phone rang and I went to get it. Shaun had given up even pretending to type and was talking to Young Nathan as if they were just sitting in a pub.

I picked up the phone and said my usual patter, both fast and slightly weary.

"Hello. How are you?"

I stopped dead.

"Oh, hi, Julia." It had been a long time. "I'm fine, thanks, and you?"

"Yes, I'm fine."

"Good. Is it Ian you're after?"

"No, Nathan if I may."

I was about to dial his extension when I glanced up and saw he wasn't at his desk. "Bear with me a moment," I said to Julia, and I put her on mute and called across to Mary, who was slicing envelopes open with a silver knife. "Is Nathan in today?"

She shook her head.

I went back to Julia. "Sorry, he's not in today. I'm not sure where he is."

"Oh, yes, of course he isn't. How silly of me."

"Well, I'm here and I didn't even realise, so don't feel too bad."

She laughed and then the line went silent for a moment. "Disappointing about the weather, isn't it?"

I looked out and the clouds still blanketed the sky, thick and off-white like heated milk. The trees looked as if they'd been cut out and superimposed on the background.

I could barely remember the bright winter blue.

"Yes," I said, "I know what you mean."

I went over to do submission at exactly three.

Each day since Shaun had started I'd had to ask him to move, and he made a big deal of dragging his body out of the chair and asking me what I wanted him to do instead.

What I really wanted him to do was figure something out so I didn't have to think of a new task each day. Every day I gave him filing as an incentive, but my scheme hadn't worked.

He groaned, but I was beyond caring and held out a wad of transmittal forms. "Don't have too much fun, now."

"I hate filing."

"Well, either you can do that or the post. I don't care which, but just entertain yourself for twenty minutes while this goes through."

"I'll file."

"Good choice."

"What are you doing, anyway?"

"Submission."

I didn't elaborate.

Ian and Young Nathan were arguing about which one of them had the more unique name. I hadn't heard of either of their surnames before I'd met them, but as their first names were quite common I said that neither was likely to be *totally* unique.

"I bet I'm the only person in the UK with my name," I said.

Ian started shuffling papers round his desk. "Pfft. I don't think so."

"Let's have a look at the database, then, shall we?" I opened all three, and did a few searches. Ian and Nathan's surnames were both in there but no one had mine.

"See?" I said, as Erica slipped behind me and into the kitchen. "I am utterly unique."

"Unique?" Erica said.

I explained to her what we were arguing about. It sounded ridiculous.

"I can do a trace if you like." She glanced up and although Big Nathan wasn't there she lowered her voice. "I can check the electoral register. Don't tell anyone, 'cause it costs the company a fiver, but I can do it."

"OK." I smiled. "Thanks."

I felt guilty because I'd started to see Erica on the train and avoid her.

I never saw her in the evening as she got a lift home from her boyfriend, but she lived somewhere between Brighton and my stop, so she was already on the train when I got on each morning.

I had no desire to speak to anyone, though, to make that stilted, bland small talk about the day; I just wanted to listen to music and let the time pass.

So I learned her habits and avoided her systematically. She always got on the front carriages as they were near the exit at the work end, so each morning I walked right down the platform to the end carriages. She must have seen me doing this, but I didn't care.

I'd walk along on the wrong side of the yellow line and hear the CrossCountry fast train coming behind me and I'd turn my head just at the moment it zipped straight through the station, feeling the air round it blowing into my face. It felt a bit like coming up on ecstasy.

And after skilfully avoiding her on the train, I'd walk behind her up the hill to work, sometimes slowing my pace so I didn't overtake her, never near enough so she had to hold the door for me.

It was Friday afternoon, and the atmosphere in the office was almost jovial. Ian and Young Nathan were sharing a joke and their laughter came floating over to us.

Mark said something and they laughed more. I watched them without really knowing why.

"What you doing next week, then?" Rachel asked.

"Sponging the mould off the walls, I should think."

"No, I mean for Valentine's Day."

I smiled. "Oh, every day is Valentine's Day for us."

"Love."

"That reminds me…" I lowered my voice. "Where is Big Nathan?"

"I don't know."

"Perhaps he's ill."

"Or abducted by aliens."

"Or kidnapped by a rogue swarm of telepathic bees."

I rang my mum that night, while I was making dinner.

"I think you need to ring the university," she said.

"Why?"

"They keep ringing here."

"Oh, do they? Sorry."

"I think they want to know what you're up to."

"I know. It's only because they want statistics for the website, so parents can see it and go, 'Ooh, eighty per cent of graduates go on to full-time work' or whatever it is."

"Okay, well, you're one of the eighty per cent, aren't you?"

"Yeah. But I didn't need a degree to become a receptionist, did I?"

"Are you applying for other jobs, then?"

"Yeah. How's Dad?"

"Oh, you know… Dad's just Dad."

"You make it sound so ominous."

"It is."

"How's Google?"

"He's okay. Always under my feet, wanting to be on the other side of the door."

"I don't know why you don't just get a cat flap."

"Come round and fit it, if you like."

"No, you're all right."

"That's probably why, then."

"Dad'll do it."

"Ha! I'd rather he got on with the kitchen. We've got two ovens now, the normal one and one in a box in the hall. It's been there so long, I put some flowers on it the other day."

"Have you dated it?"

"I certainly have."

When we were growing up she got into a habit of writing the date that Dad started a job in felt tip somewhere, so she could keep track of how long it took him to finish. She waited for wallpaper in the front room for four years.

"I don't know why you don't just do it yourself," I said.

"I could do. I could do, but it's his part of the bargain, isn't it?"

"Bargain?"

"Yeah. You know, marriage and that."

"It's a bargain, is it?"

"In some ways, yes." She paused. "Poor Dad."

*

I hadn't been lying about the mould.

For a week or so I had noticed the patches I had sponged off before Christmas starting to darken through the cheap emulsion again. It was especially bad in the bedroom, but none of the rooms were free of it and the place smelt clammy, like a cold armpit.

Water dripped down the inside of the windows each morning, so I had taken Clive's advice and got into the habit of drying them with an old green towel while I did my teeth. All the Traffic Warden did was wipe sweaty arcs so he could see what was going on outside.

I filled a bucket with warm water and got the mould killer from under the sink, and started in the bedroom. The Traffic Warden was still in bed, reading his new laptop magazine.

"I think I know what desktop computer we should get," he said. "When we settle down."

"Settle down?"

"Yeah, you know. With kids, we'll want a big screen, and —"

"Are you going to give us a hand with this, then?" I asked.

"Just leave some for me, and I'll do it later."

"Are you actually going to do it, or are you just saying that?"

He put the magazine down. "Give us a break, will you? This is the first Saturday I've had off in ages."

"So? You've had other days off. What's the difference if it's Saturday?"

"Can I not just be left to relax?"

I climbed on a chair so I could reach into the corner. "Don't you find it easier to relax when you've got all your chores done?"

"I find it easier to relax when I don't have some bint chewing my ear off."

"All right, cunt." I squeezed the sponge over my bucket and watched the water go cloudy. "Sounds like Valentine's Day is going to be fun."

"Oh, yes, the day of love. You know, I'm so glad that we don't buy into any of that crap. I'm so glad you're not a typical woman and we don't have to pretend."

I sprayed the mould killer into the corner of the ceiling and it floated into my eyes.

When I'd finished in the bedroom I started on the living room, which meant I had to move the dining table, and as I did, a stack of old bills and papers slid onto the floor. That was when I found the photo.

It was one of my favourite photos, and had been tacked up on the wall of my student bedroom. I hadn't even realised it was missing in the flat.

It was of us two, taken on the back of a ferry at night.

I remembered being there. When we were students eight of us had gone to France to get as much booze as we could, and while everyone else had been happy to stay inside amongst the chintz and sterile furnishings, the Traffic Warden had wanted to go outside. I'd felt like I was going to puke any minute, so I'd followed him out into the salty wind, and we had slipped about on the wet deck in our flip-flops, hardly daring to let go of the railing, like two crisp packets in a storm. Someone in the group must have followed us out and taken the picture.

We were both wearing black jumpers so our heads looked disembodied in the photograph, except I was wearing a rainbow pashmina. I had let my hair loose from its usual ponytail and in the wind it was flying upwards. I remembered how it felt, snapping at my face.

We'd only known each other for two months or so when it had been taken, but it was clear that we were going to be more than friends. Somehow we just looked as if we were made of the same stuff.

We looked like we didn't give a fuck about anything.

I opened the window of the lounge and all I could hear was the drone of a distant mower.

I rubbed my thumb over our faces, as if the answers were there somewhere.

In the afternoon, we drove to the supermarket. "We must be mad," I said, as we pulled into the car park. "It'll be packed."

The Traffic Warden talked about old people, and how they went shopping at the weekend even though they had the whole of the rest of the week to go, when everyone else was working.

I looked out of the window. The blankness of the sky made me feel as if my own insides were turning grey. I felt as if I was living in a cupboard. I felt like a peg being hammered into the ground.

"Remind me that we need cotton buds," I said.

The Traffic Warden said, "I think I've got cancer."

"Why?" I asked.

"Keep getting up to go to the toilet. I never used to do that."

"So?"

"First sign of prostate cancer." He paused, and we both watched an old woman who was hunched over her trolley at a ninety-degree angle. "I feel like I'm dying sometimes."

"Perhaps it's a sign of contentment," I said.

"Wife Beater?"

"No."

And he meant it. I didn't know how I could tell; I just could.

"Are you going to get yourself checked out, then?" I squeezed a tomato.

"What?"

"If you're worried. Get yourself checked."

"Maybe."

I put the tomatoes in the trolley. "Well, don't come running to me when you're dead."

"Don't worry, I won't."

"Are you going to get any veg, then, or just stand there?"

He went off and I lost him, and walked around on my own with the trolley.

I wandered round the Fruit 'n' Veg section. All the different shapes and colours and tastes seemed so appealing, like heaps of jewels, and I wanted to take them all home.

I searched through a box of peppers, testing them, feeling their smooth skins in my hand. I hated finding any fruits or vegetables that were slightly deformed – carrots that were fused together like a pair of legs, or apples with brown patches – because I knew that they wouldn't be sold. Sometimes I felt so sorry for them that I bought them on principle. I must be the only person in the world who feels sorry for fruit.

At the checkout, the girl in front of us loaded her shopping into a canvas bag with some dancing runner beans on the side and a speech bubble that said, *It's Good To Be Green*. I looked into her face and tried to figure out if she thought she was saving the world.

It was impossible to tell.

We carried the bags half-half from the boot to the flat, but the Traffic Warden did his usual trick of leaving his load in the hallway. I took it into the kitchen and the fridge motor stopped and it was suddenly silent.

I stood and listened.

And there it was, again.

For a few weeks, I had been hearing white noise in the flat. It was so faint: a distant buzz behind the walls like music through headphones that you aren't wearing, or a phone ringing in the next house along.

As if something restless was there.

"I'll put the shopping away, then," I said, purely to make some other sound.

The Traffic Warden stood in the lounge. "I don't mind doing it."

"Yes, but unfortunately you haven't a clue where anything goes."

"Of course I do."

"No, you don't."

There was a long pause, and then he called through, "She's getting plump."

"Who?"

He was looking out the lounge window, so I went over. Mini Man and his girlfriend were standing in the street, both smoking. Their kid was with them in her pyjamas, sugar pink and spotted with balloons. She was dragging a blanket or something on the ground, and starting to grizzle.

"Stop it, Jessica." The girlfriend. She sounded so exhausted. "Don't start now, or you'll go to bed straight away."

"She's not plump. She's pregnant."

"Hey – she's Mini Mum."

I smiled. "Yeah." I tapped the closed door of the washing machine with my foot. "Your washing's done."

"Thanks." He started pulling it out.

For a long time when I'd first moved in, he had left piles of wet laundry around the flat, but since his favourite T-shirt had got mildew he'd started to hang stuff up straight away, developing the equally annoying habit of putting all his shirts on hangers and drying them in doorways as he was convinced that he had to dry them in the quickest way possible.

"Got any hangers?" he asked.

I turned out of the fridge and patted my pockets. "Not on me, no."

"Very funny."

"I keep them in the wardrobe." I reached to put tins in the cupboard. "You know me and my funny habits." As he went off to the bedroom I called through, "Can we not have stuff hanging in every doorway, though?"

He turned back. "Why not?"

"Why? Why can't you just use the airer like everyone else?"

"Why can't you just shut up like everyone else?"

"*Because* every time I walk through a doorway they fall off, so every time I move around I have to spend half an hour picking them up. It's irritating."

"Don't be stupid."

"Imagine how annoyed you'd be if I hung bead curtains in all the doorways."

"I wouldn't give a shit."

"Don't lie. You would and we both know it."

He didn't answer, and then I heard the clattering of hangers.

*

I did my teeth and got into bed, and he flicked the light out.

I reached into my bedside drawer and pulled out a little torch that his mum had given me for Christmas.

He groaned and rolled over. "That's so bright."

I said nothing. It produced a small pool of light over what I was reading; the rest of the room was pitch black. I wondered briefly if it was worse to hit someone than to really want to.

His breathing relaxed and I hoped he was sleeping so he wouldn't go on the next day about me keeping him up.

After about half an hour I turned the light off, put my book down and closed my eyes for sleep.

As if someone had uttered a spell he was awake, and ran his hand over my breast. I snuggled into his warmth. Our lips found each other's. He whispered, "Let me fuck you," before tugging at my pants.

We had sex and neither of us said a word.

I dug my nails into his back as if I was clinging to the mud of a cliff top, worried I would fall off.

He pulled out just before he came.

We checked the sheet for come by passing our hands across it. I didn't want to roll into any goo once it was cold. I found my pants, twisted into a thick white band by the bed, and went to the bathroom.

My eyes seemed dark in the mirror.

When I was back I put my face on his shoulder and my cold feet on his legs and wondered how it was I could feel lonely and loved at the same time.

*

On Monday morning I got to work to find Mark the IT guy and Ian, both with their hands on their hips, looking at the parts of the new desks laid out on the floor.

I grinned at Rachel. "Shall we do a sweepstake? I call lunch."

She snorted. "That's ambitious."

"Need a hand?" I asked Mark.

He frowned, but didn't take his eyes off the parts. "No. Thanks all the same."

All morning I entered data and listened to Ian and Mark. "That's not a bracket. I know a bracket when I see one." "Oh, hang on a minute, that's the wrong way round."

I enjoyed being distracted from listening to Shaun wittering on to Young Nathan about the Vauxhall Nova he wanted to get and how drunk he'd been at the weekend.

"What if they separate us?" Rachel asked.

Ruth leaned over and whispered, "They won't."

"Really?"

"Yes. They asked me and I said that you talk, but work at the same time. Unlike some other people I could mention."

"Is he coming over?" I asked.

"Yes, well, it makes sense for you two to be together, doesn't it?"

"I suppose so."

At lunch I went to Londis and was served by Bobby again, so I said hello. I couldn't tell if he recognised me but I think he did. He called me Madam a lot again.

When I got back to the office I found that they'd crushed all the customer service desks together and moved them up, cutting off the walkway up the back by the filing cabinets.

I was surprised when Mark turned around and said, "Where do you want to sit?"

"Next to Rachel."

"Really?"

"Yup."

Ian pushed his glasses up his nose. "Women. Love to yak."

I smiled at him, saccharine. "Not my fault if she's the only sentient being here."

I was moved from being opposite Rachel to next to her, so now I had my back to the window and a view of the whole office. I had to tuck my chair right in before anyone could walk behind me. It felt a bit like the walls were inching in.

In the afternoon Mark started to hook up my computer, so I put my phone through to Mary and went up the back to do some filing.

"Do you wanna do some of mine?" Rachel asked, when she saw me putting my sheets in alphabetical order. Last week she'd hidden her pile under her desk as it was over one foot tall, and she was worried that Big Nathan would see it.

"Yeah, go on then."

She perked up. "Really?"

"Ha! No."

When Mark was done with my computer, he started to set up one on the desk opposite me, and Shaun came across, bringing his red Arsenal beanie bear and his Arsenal mug with him.

"Now the data entry department can be together," Mark said.

I smiled, tight-lipped. "Hooray."

I had wondered if there was something about Young Nathan that made Shaun constantly chat, but after an hour I realised that it wouldn't have mattered if he'd had a scarecrow opposite him. He just talked.

On our second day of sitting opposite each other I started to time how long he'd talk if I kept working and didn't respond to him at all. The longest was seven minutes, and he only stopped because he went to make a cup of tea.

I heard about his mate's eyebrow piercing, about how he'd got fired from a bakery, and then he started on the skids he had done or could do on his moped.

"Shaun," I said, cutting him off mid-sentence. "I'm not being funny, but you're not in school. You're being paid to be here, so you need to actually do some work."

"You're strict."

"Just get on with it."

"You remind me of this teacher I had, Mrs Crowther. One time I was in Maths, yeah..."

"Shaun." I mimed typing.

"Okay, boss woman." And he started pecking at the keyboard.

"I'm not your boss."

I looked over at Big Nathan's chair, and it was still empty.

When I went over to do submission that afternoon, I asked

Mary.

"He's gone for a knee operation," she said, as if it was obvious.

"When is he back?"

"Next week."

Young Nathan looked up from his computer, grinning. "Enjoying your new colleague?"

I'd sent Shaun up the back to do some filing, so I didn't need to lower my voice, but I gave him the finger anyway.

He cupped his hands round his ears. "Oh, I'm sorry, I was too busy enjoying the blissful silence."

Mary and Ian were laughing.

"Yes, yes, very funny, thank you all for your solidarity."

"You can count on us," Ian said.

"Check this out," Young Nathan said, and he held up a Bic biro.

"It's a pen."

"Yeah, but it's got no ink. See? Clear barrel." He scribbled on his pad and held it out.

"Magic."

"Well, I think it's cool."

"Whatever gets you through the day. Speaking of which, how is the novel going?"

He sighed and I wished I'd kept my mouth shut.

"*Nana*," I said quickly. "Have you finished it yet?"

"Oh. No, I don't think I've read any since we last spoke about it, actually."

"Enjoying it then, huh?"

"Yes, thanks, just busy having a life."

"Yeah, 'cause you're so popular and cool."

Ian laughed.

There was a long silence while I waited for the MRP

162

submission to go through. Young Nathan went back to typing.

"What do you think the ICS submission's going to be?" I asked.

"How would I know? The numbers are random."

"Sort of, but not really. Presumably it's based on how many I've input that day."

"Don't you mean 'we' now that you have an inputting companion?"

I smiled. "No." I tapped the pile of grey forms on the desk. "I'm going to go with... one forty."

"A hundred and—"

"Don't say forty-one."

"Forty-two."

"Don't be annoying."

"You said to guess."

"All right, what do you reckon CRS will be?"

"I really have no idea."

"It is more random. But guess."

"A hundred."

"That's way off."

He pointed his magic pen at me. "This is not really fair. You've seen the numbers that come up every day."

"Oh, stop whining. I'm going to say... ninety-nine."

Young Nathan won the first and I won the second.

*

When I got back to the flat I hovered my key over the lock to see if the door would snap open, but nothing happened.

He was smoking by the window. "Have you called the doctor yet?" I asked.

"What for?"

"To get checked out. For whatever life-threatening disease you're certain to have."

"He'll think I'm a hypochondriac."

"So what?"

He said nothing.

I pulled my work shirt over my head and stood in the doorway in my bra. "Since when have you cared about what people think of you, anyway?"

"I don't really, but I don't want to waste his time."

"How many tickets'd you give out today?"

"Three."

I went to the bedroom, and put on a T-shirt and my pyjama trousers. "So, you're just going to live in fear, then?"

"Oh, give it up."

I held my hands up. "Okay. I'm not your mum."

"No, you're not, and I don't need another."

I went to put the oven on for dinner. "Could have fucking fooled me."

*

We went to bed.

I had started reading a book by Charles Bukowski that the Traffic Warden had finished the week before. He was back to reading *What Laptop?* magazine.

I closed the Bukowski and looked at the cover. "I can't believe you liked this book."

"Why not? It's funny."

"It's like some pathetic teenage male fantasy. The guy is ugly, alcoholic and fifty-five, and we're meant to believe that woman after woman falls over herself to be with him."

"So?"

"So, I mean, he doesn't even *seduce* them. There's no romance, not even persuasion, nothing, but it's all set up like a memoir, as if it's true and really happened that way! It's a fucking joke."

He shrugged. "It's possible."

"Oh, you've got to be kidding me. Tell you what: ring me when you're fifty-five and tell me how much sex you're having."

"Well, Charles Bukowski *was* a famous recluse. So the only people he really came into contact with were fans."

"So lots of young women sought him out, but not one of them was disappointed? I'm sure that more than one would have built him up in their mind to be some dishy maverick and then found the reality to be so totally different... Come on, you know that sex is an absolute minefield, yet there's never a moment of even the slightest embarrassment, or rejection, or anything." I picked it up as if to read again, but put the book back down. "And the worst part is that if he was a woman, it'd be called *Diary of a Slag*. But he just says, 'Hey, look at me, I'm a complete arsehole and I can have sex with any woman I want with no repercussions and I don't care about any of them because I'm just too cool.'"

The Traffic Warden shrugged again. "Okay, so you don't like the book."

I really wanted him to fight with me, to affirm or change what I thought, but he wouldn't bite. I wondered if there had been a time when he would have argued with me, but I couldn't remember.

I sighed and turned away, putting the book by the bed. "No, I don't like the book."

I looked at the ceiling for a while and then turned to face him on the pillow. "Do you ever worry that I'll go off with someone else?"

"Not really."

"Thanks."

"There's no point worrying about something like that. Especially when there's nothing I can do to stop you."

"How do you know?"

"Know what?" He still hadn't put the magazine down, even though we both knew he couldn't have been reading it while we were talking.

"How do you know that there's nothing you can do to stop me?"

"Because if you're gonna do it then you're gonna do it. End of story."

"Ooh, how romantic." This was coming from a man who used to go into a frenzy at the very mention of one of my exes.

He turned the page in his magazine, and pulled the duvet over to his side more. "I'm starting to think I'd be glad of the peace."

I pulled the covers back. "Sorry that a conversation with me is such an imposition."

"I can't win with you, can I?"

I looked at the ceiling. "You used to be so passionate about…" I was going to say *me* or *us*, but I chickened out. "Stuff."

"I still am."

"About what? Laptops? What Mini Man's wearing this week?"

"Actually, this is a very interesting magazine."

I wanted to fight. I wanted to know that there was something burning under the surface of everything else, and fighting seemed the only way to do it.

"Well, I can see it's more interesting than a conversation with me." I turned away and closed my eyes as if to sleep, thinking he might copy. I switched my bedside lamp off, making the room black.

"Oi."

I didn't respond.

"Oi, put the light back on."

I turned it back on. "It's usually me who has to beg you to have the light on."

I pretended to sleep and thought of all the times we'd had this argument and why I always lost.

A while later I heard him put the magazine down and shuffle down in the bed. I didn't want him to know I was awake, so I didn't move, and felt him reaching across me for the lamp.

I was facing away from him and he spooned around me, and I felt his hand starting to rub my breasts. I heard his breathing quicken and felt his erection on my arse as he pressed himself hard into me. I thought he was trying to wake me, so I stirred slightly, but he stopped moving, so I stayed perfectly still and imagined that I was a sleeping woman in a fairy tale.

*

One morning, I was walking up the hill from the station to work when I went under a road sign held up by two thick poles. For some reason I imagined the sign coming loose and slipping down the poles, cutting my head like a melon under a guillotine.

I saw the cross-section of my skull, the white line of the bone and the red spilling into a pool on the pavement.

Now Shaun had officially "settled in", I went back to my usual twelve o'clock lunches.

"You going on lunch now?" Rachel asked. "I'll miss you."

"Well, I'll teach Shaun the phones soon, so hopefully we'll do it half-half."

"Teaching me the phones?" Shaun said, looking up.

"Yup."

The disadvantage of swapping about lunchtimes was that, despite the fact that I was eating my sandwiches, Ian spoke to me about work for three minutes during my lunch hour.

I couldn't go back at 13.03 because Mary wanted to go up the town and passed the phone back to me at exactly one o'clock. Instead, I went to the stationery cupboard, and took a small box of staples.

Although they had cost the company no more than thirty pence, they would have cost me at least a pound in the shop, so I felt that it was another day squared with the world.

On the way home I walked down the platform on the wrong side of the yellow line. A freight train shot past and made my unbuttoned trench coat billow outwards like a cape, and I imagined one of the buttons getting caught somehow and me being dragged along between the train and the tracks until there were bits of me scattered for miles.

I didn't stop at my usual spot, but kept going, past the other commuters and out of the shelter.

I thought of an old TV programme where a guy played pranks on the public, like tying a bunch of helium balloons to a fake baby and filming horrified onlookers as it floated off. One of my favourite sketches was when he dressed as the Grim Reaper and stood with his scythe on a windy hill, next to a generic rail sign that said *Nowhere*.

When I was on the train I looked out of my window for him. I wanted to see something tangible that other people were missing, but of course he wasn't there.

*

"She is *huge*."

168

We were watching Mini Man and Mini Mum in the courtyard out the back. He kept jumping in the Mini, fiddling with something under the steering wheel, and leaping out again.

"She's not that big. About six months, I reckon." She was smoking.

Jessica was wandering around, swinging a green toy rabbit by the ears.

"Looks like he's finished," the Traffic Warden said.

Just as he said it, the engine revved, and Mini Mum let out a muted cheer.

"Wow."

"What?"

"She smiled."

"Has she changed her hair again?" I asked. "She changes it so often I can never tell."

"I think she's a hairdresser."

"I never see her going anywhere, though."

"She works from home."

"Well, I guess she can choose her own hours that way. Be hard with two kids, though."

"When we have babies, I'm not having you working."

"You're not—" I closed my mouth, then opened it again, but I didn't know where to start. I looked at the Traffic Warden as if I'd never met him. "I'm sorry, do I know you? Actually, do you know me? *At all*? Perhaps we met at the time warp party, just after we left the caves—"

"Come on, you know I didn't mean—" He stopped, to his credit, and let me have my moment.

I started beating my fists against my chest and doing a caveman impression. "Me man. You woman. Clean house. Cook dinner. Have baby."

"Look, it's just that I want to be in a position where one of us can stay at home before we have kids, that's all."

"And you've decided that that person is me?"

"Well, I assumed you'd *want* to stay at home. You love babies and kittens and stuff."

I rubbed my eyes. I knew I was making a cheap shot, but I didn't know what else to do. "Well, I do have a better degree than you and at least some ambition, so don't take me out of the running just yet, eh?"

"I didn't mean it like that—"

I moved away from the window. "I'll start dinner, then." I thought he might offer to cook and atone in some way for his misdemeanour, but he stayed by the window.

I went to the kitchen and starting taking stuff out of the fridge. I *willed* him to come. I willed him to come and take the pan out of my hand and to pick me up and throw me over his shoulder and make me see the funny side of that whole conversation so it could be wiped clean.

*

"Hey."

Young Nathan looked up. "Hey."

"Good weekend?"

"'S all right. You?"

"Yeah, not bad."

There was a pause while I waited for submission to load up.

"Do you want to hear something really pathetic?" Young Nathan asked.

"God, yes."

"On Saturday I went into Waterstone's not to buy anything, but just to look at the space where my book would be. I just wanted to see it, to imagine my book there."

"What's so pathetic about that?"

"Well, it's the book I haven't written because I choose to spend my time doing things like that."

"Oh. Thought it was going to be a bit juicier than that. Numbers?"

Due to a heated discussion the previous week, we'd taken to writing our submission predictions down on our respective notepads, so there was no disagreement and negotiation.

"I have something to show you, too," he said.

"What?"

"You're going to like this." He started turning his monitor round.

It was a colour-coded bar graph of wins at the submission game.

"Busy morning, was it?"

He coughed and Ian smirked. "Fairly, actually. Took me two seconds to knock this baby up."

"Okay, now that *is* pathetic."

Rachel said she didn't feel well and went home at four, and Shaun spent the last hour going on about how she was a MILF. He spoke in a low voice as if we were conspiring and I was remotely interested, but I tuned him out until he said, "I'd really like to fuck the shit out of her."

I sighed. "Put a sock in it, Shaun, for the love of God."

"What?"

"I'm really not interested, okay? She's my mate."

"Yeah, and she's fit."

I decided to get him on the phones there and then. At least then he'd be able to talk to someone other than me.

It occurred to me that Big Nathan probably didn't think I'd

ever teach Shaun to do anything but data input, but I'd read his job description and it was exactly the same as mine, so I didn't see why not.

I told Shaun exactly what Mel had told me. "Okay. If you cut someone off, don't worry because they'll call right back."

Young Nathan was just walking past on his way to the filing cabinets when he heard me say that, and he sniggered. "There speaks a true receptionist."

"Haven't you got any graphs to create?" I turned back to Shaun and pointed out the different buttons. "So if you need to ask me something without them hearing, press 'Mute'. This arrow transfers it across so you can put it through to someone else, and this one will bring it back to you, but I'll show you how to do that when you have to. These are the holds, one, two, and three—"

He wasn't listening.

"Okay, so I'll leave that with you, then." I turned the phone round so it faced him, and he looked at it as if it was going to bite him.

After a long debate we split up phone work so I would do mornings and Shaun afternoons, and we took it in turns to cover the lunch time so every other day I could go on lunch at one.

The next day I went to the park with Rachel for lunch. It wasn't particularly warm but it didn't look like rain. The air outside was as stuffy as inside the office, where the windows tilted outwards but didn't open more than three inches.

"Can I ask you something?" she said.

"You're going to anyway, but yes."

"Do you fancy Young Nathan?"

"No."

"Really?"

"Yeah." I bit into my sandwich. "I can see why you'd think it, but... no."

"I think he fancies you."

"I think it's irrelevant. There are a lot of reasons we're not compatible. Can you imagine arguing with the guy? I'd cut his fucking head off."

"True. And sorry for asking, in a way, because you're obviously happy as you are."

"Oh, yes, I'm ecstatic."

"Trouble in paradise?"

I didn't really know how to answer. "Why don't you live with a man?"

"I can't. I did try once, with Amy's dad." She remembered and waved her hand. "No, not for me. I like things my way."

"Don't you miss having someone around?"

"I have someone around."

"Apart from Amy."

"There is no one apart from Amy."

"I know, but you know one day she'll leave home."

She grimaced. "Oh, don't. I can't bear it."

"Have you got smoked salmon sandwiches?"

"Yeah."

"I love smoked salmon. It's one of my favourite things in the world."

"Me too. But no, the truth about men is that I don't need one. I miss having sex sometimes, but I can't bear living with them. I *love* being independent. I sacrifice nothing, for nobody."

"Not all men want you to sacrifice something, though."

"No, they don't *want* you to because they don't have to want you to. They know you're going to do it. I mean, who wouldn't want a wife? I know I could put one to good use."

We chewed our sandwiches.

She shivered.

"Are you okay?" I asked.

"Not really, but I will be."

"What's up?"

"Do you want to go out for a drink later in the week? I'll take Amy to my mum's or something."

"Okay, sure."

"Here." She held out a rubbish bag and I put my ball of foil and apple core inside.

"Thanks."

"So," she said. "Shaun."

"Oh my God, don't get me started. What is it with that kid? I mean, is he ever going to shut the fuck up? I really don't understand what Big Nathan was thinking when he hired him."

"He talks. He does talk. But he's harmless."

"Maybe, but *I* won't be if he keeps talking. I'll strangle him, I swear. Still, hopefully it won't be for much longer."

"Why?"

"I have another interview."

"Congratulations! What is it for?"

"It's for a junior editor on a magazine. A total long shot, but it's really well-paid."

"Well, good for you. And good luck! Though I hope you don't get it. Who am I going to talk to?"

I smiled. "Shaun."

"I said, 'Who am I going to talk to?', not 'Who's going to talk at me?'"

We got up and brushed the grass off our clothes.

"How's my arse?" she asked.

"Grass-free. Mine?"

"Yep."

"Good. I hope this weather lets up soon. I don't care if it rains. I just need a bit of variation. What is with these clouds? Every day is the same."

"I can't *wait* for summer. Which reminds me, nearly time to go to the tanning salon."

"Tanning salon? Are you serious? Actually, don't answer that. But for the record, you wanna get your head checked."

"No, I want to get myself brown as a nut."

She lit a fag.

"Good idea." I lit one too.

We walked up the hill not saying anything.

"Well, back in we go."

"Yep."

I went to see Big Nathan that afternoon.

I had dressed up slightly, but I wasn't sure if it was coincidence. Normally my clothes were slightly on the casual side, but I was just young and stupid enough to get away with it. Only Kelly, Erica and I had this bizarre honour.

I didn't want him to think I was his efficient little secretary, so I stood with my arms folded and a bunch of papers bent in my hand that may or may not have been important.

"Hello," I said.

He looked up from his laptop. "Hello." He said it to me like I was a friend of his daughter's, come over for tea.

"How's it going?"

"Good, thanks."

"Good. Um… I need to take a few hours next Friday. I'll probably need to go about three…"

"Okay."

"I have a dentist appointment."

"Okay."

"I'll make up the time." I bit my lip.

He was still smiling. "Okay."

"Right. Thanks." I went to walk away.

"How's Shaun getting on?"

I shrugged. "The force is not strong in the young one."

He stared at me and then laughed.

So did I.

Rachel's mobile buzzed on the desk, vibrating along on the laminated wood. Usually she answered it there and then, which I liked because her side of the conversation always sounded so cryptic I could never tell who she was talking to or what the call was about.

This time she saw who was calling, put her office phone on divert, and took it outside. I heard, "Oh, God," just as the door shut behind her.

"What's up with her?" Shaun asked.

"I don't know."

He started talking about some girl he'd seen at the weekend and I tuned him out and watched the door. I knew something was wrong, and was trying to think if Rachel had said anything that should've registered with me but hadn't.

Fifteen minutes passed. I wondered if I should get up and go outside on pretences of going to the toilet, but I thought she might want privacy and I didn't want to invade it for my own selfish curiosity.

After twenty minutes, she came back in without making eye contact with anyone, packed her stuff into her bag, turned off her computer, and asked Ruth in a mumble whether she could have two minutes outside.

I was so surprised I said nothing but just watched, helpless, as they went out the office.

Five minutes later, Ruth came back in, without Rachel.

I watched her sit back down.

"What's going on?" Shaun asked.

"Get on with your work," Ruth said.

He went to make a cup of tea, and Ruth leaned over to me. "Thought you might want to know, Rachel's father died. I suppose you know he was sick."

"Oh, right, yes, of course," I said.

I wanted Ruth to think Rachel and I were better friends than we really were. Maybe I wanted to be a better friend than I really was. I sent Rachel a text, to say that I knew and I was sorry, and if she or Amy needed anything I was there.

She didn't reply.

*

The Traffic Warden was on an early and we both woke up at his alarm. I cuddled him in the grey morning light and he stroked my hair.

Someone outside started revving their car engine.

"Why does this place seem to be full of dickheads?" he asked.

"I don't know."

"I don't want to get up."

"I know."

After he left I got in the shower, and that's when I started to hear the screams.

I rinsed quickly and stepped out, and stood near the flat door in my towel. It was definitely coming from the hallway, which amplified sound by ten. It was *ungodly*. Like someone being murdered.

Like a child.

I put my hand on the door handle, but then thought that I couldn't really go up there in just a towel, so I took it off again.

And waited.

Then the screams stopped.

Rachel wasn't in and Shaun kept going on about it.

He asked me if he could go on lunch at one even though it wasn't his turn. The truth was that without Rachel there I didn't really care one way or the other, but I said yes as if I was really reluctant because I knew he'd start doing it all the time if I didn't.

At twelve, I went to the park and sat under the grey clouds by myself.

I looked at the clouds, and wondered if the world had already ended, and now we were in hell. It would make sense. The myth of the afterlife is all set out wrong: heaven doesn't exist, and limbo is worse than hell.

*

As I got to the main door of our flat, I saw the Traffic Warden's face in the window, and when he saw me he opened the window, leaned out, and belched into the air.

I laughed, until I noticed a shadow moving behind the net curtains in Mike's flat, below.

The Traffic Warden had a new video game, *Halo*, and he taught me how to play. As little gunmen we climbed mountains and picked up weapons, looked for cover and shot at robots.

I wasn't very good and kept getting shot, and then had to wait to respawn. "Wouldn't it be cool if you could respawn in real life?"

"Fucking brilliant," he said, and then about the game, "Don't die again."

"If you got the chance to live your life over, what mistakes would you avoid?"

"You."

"Thanks."

"You're going to die."

I wasn't looking at the screen. "What?"

And then we watched my character getting shot and falling to the ground and my screen turning red.

"Hey, I haven't asked you – how many tickets'd you give out today?"

"Two."

"Only two?"

"You've respawned."

We'd been playing for a little while when we went up a canyon in search of the next level. It was a desolate place, and the Traffic Warden nearly stepped on a bridge that snapped like a bone.

"Apocalyptic," I said.

"Have this for an apocalypse." He shot at me, so I shot back, and then we started spraying each other with bullets.

By pure fluke I nearly had the Traffic Warden, but just stopped short of killing him. After he had fully regenerated, he fired at me until I was dead.

Then he said, "Truce."

After dinner he was washing up, wiping the curve of the wok with the wrong side of the sponge.

I crept up behind him on the tiles and put my arms round his middle, inside his T-shirt. I rubbed his stomach, thick with hair.

"Is yer belly sore where the pig bit ya?"

"*Shhh.*"

With a soapy finger, he turned the volume up on the little silver radio. The lady on it was talking about prostate cancer.

I stepped away from him, got the milk out and drank from the bottle. As we both did it and always had done, there didn't seem a lot of point in breaking the habit.

The dried bits of milk round the top stuck to my lips.

I wandered out, as if I was trying to remember why I'd come, though not before I heard him say, "I'm going to get it checked out."

*

By the following Friday, Rachel still wasn't back.

Ruth was struggling in customer service as Kyle was on holiday, and she asked me to do the stage fours for her, which meant going through a computer-generated list of people who needed to be sent a reminder letter. The letter was saved on the system as a template, but I had to go through each version, meticulously checking the account, the amounts and dates, and print each one off separately, so it took me all day.

The job itself was no more monotonous than data entry, but because I wasn't inputting I felt like I had done no work.

As I stood at the enveloping machine, I realised that I had spent the day alone, but in a room full of people.

I was due to leave early for my interview, so I did submission at two thirty. Young Nathan was typing away but had, as usual, nothing in front of him. I asked him once where all his work was, and he smiled, pointed to his computer screen and then tapped his forehead.

"How's your day been?" he asked.

"All right. I did about eight pages of stage fours."

"Fun for you."

I lowered my voice. "It reminds me of that myth, you know, the guy who has to roll a boulder up a hill and then watch it roll down, on and on, forever?"

"Sisyphus."

"Is that it? I thought I was in one of the circles of Hell."

He smiled. "Got my numbers ready."

"Excitement of the day."

We both paused.

"Truly."

"Have you heard anything from Rachel?" Mary asked.

"No. I texted her, but she didn't reply. I'm a bit worried, actually."

"Of course you are. You must miss your little friend." She said it as if I was a child who'd lost their teddy, and it made me wonder if Rachel had been a figment of my imagination all this time, a split personality I'd created to deal with the office.

*

The interview started at three thirty, but the office was hidden from the road, so I walked past it a few times and arrived five minutes late. The building was called the Old Waxworks and was made of crumbling red brick with plants clinging to it. The door was heavy wood and came to a point at the top, like the door of a church.

Inside was fairly dark and smelled like cedar, but it had modern steel light fixtures and a few black square chairs and some of the place's own magazines laid out on a low coffee table.

The receptionist sat behind a large oak desk, and I introduced myself, breathless. Since becoming a receptionist myself I'd always been super-nice to them, but it didn't register with this one at all and she looked at me with her head on one side and her eyes narrowed, as if I was a distasteful abstract painting she didn't understand.

"Take a seat, then, please."

And she turned back to her computer.

After five minutes it was obvious that my interviewer was running late, so I sat there feeling like some fancy, curvy piece of furniture until he appeared. He had jeans and a soft blue collared shirt on, and as soon as he saw me he started to go bright red, which I felt gave me the upper hand.

"We're in the attic, I'm afraid," he explained, and I followed him through a crooked corridor. "So there's a few stairs to climb." The staircase was spiral and wrought iron, so I could see the ground through the lattice.

The attic had a sloping roof right over one side, but there was room for eight separate desks, some with drawing boards beside them. There were sagging shelves of books all over the place, stacks of magazines and posters pinned to the wooden beams, spider plants trailing over everything, and a few velvet bean bags in the corner.

I wanted the job about twice as much.

"Well, this is where it all happens. Not very exciting, I know."

"Oh, no, it is."

He raised his eyebrows. "O-kay."

"No, really," I said. "The office I work in at the moment is very... generic."

"Right. Well, I guess you just get used to whatever's around."

I looked at the desk beside me, where there was a pile of different paper aeroplanes.

We carried on through the office, down another corridor that I had to duck through, and into a private room. The interviewer sat down and motioned for me to do the same.

"So." He had my CV and looked down it. "At the moment you work at… Weblands."

"Yes."

"You're a… data inputter. Sounds…" He smiled. "Interesting."

"It's not. I mean, I've improved my typing skills and I have developed a good eye for detail, which I guess would be useful for this job, but it's not my life's ambition, no."

"What is your life's ambition?"

I paused. "Well, truthfully, I'm not sure. I don't have a set idea about it. But I know that I want to do something that requires a bit of creativity. I want to be able to pick up new skills."

"OK. Sorry, perhaps that was an unfair question. I have too much coffee in my system, I think."

I just smiled, wordless.

"So, you went to university. How was that?"

"Great. I learnt lots."

"Like what?"

"Well, I learnt a lot about language—"

"Of course you did, it was an English degree. What else?"

I opened my mouth and closed it again. I thought maybe he'd interrupt to retract the question and save me. But he didn't.

"I'm sorry, I don't know what you mean."

He leaned forward. "It was a simple question." With each word he stabbed the table with his pen. "What. Did. You. Learn?"

There was something threatening in his manner, but I couldn't tell if it was genuine or just me being sensitive. A pause grew in the room.

I swallowed. "I don't know."

And I knew it was over.

I waited until I got home before I cried, but I had stopped by the time the Traffic Warden got in, and started dinner.

"How'd it go?"

"It was the worst interview ever." I told him about it. He gave me a hug and I put my nose deep into his uniform sweatshirt. He smelled like pasties and fag smoke.

"The guy sounds like a total cunt, so perhaps you're better off without it."

"That's what I thought at first, but maybe he just wanted to rattle me a bit."

"Don't take it so personally…"

"But it *is* fucking personal. It's my fucking *life*…"

"I'm sure it wasn't that bad."

"It was. The silence in the room was so thick I could taste it. He thought I was a fucking idiot."

"Well, don't let it get to you. Just move on."

I stepped away from him. "How can I? How can I just move on when I mess up a chance at the perfect job, and I'm going to be stuck at Weblands for the rest of my life?"

"You won't be there forever."

"How do you know? Maybe I will be. What if I'm there in another six months? What then? In another year? Should I just kill myself now, get it over with?"

I went out of the kitchen and fumbled in my bag for my cigarettes, took one out and lit it.

"Well, I haven't got the solution."

"I don't want you to have the solution."

"I don't know what to say." He scratched the back of his head. For the first time since I'd known him, he looked uncomfortable. I turned away. It was, to use a word of my mother's, *unbearable*.

"Look, I don't think that there is a solution. I just want you to understand. I feel so... fucking *restless*, you know? More and more I think, *Is this it? Is this all there's ever going to be?*"

He said nothing.

I felt I should shut up, but I didn't. "It's like I'm wasting away, and if I don't do something soon I'm going to die being totally dissatisfied with my life. Don't you ever feel that way?"

He opened his mouth to answer, but before he said anything the screaming started again.

I was almost relieved because at least it meant the girl was still alive, but my relief didn't last long.

"What the hell is that?" he asked.

"It's the same as what I heard the other morning."

I stubbed my fag out and we stood in the hallway together, listening to it. I was glad he was there.

"It's got to be number nine."

"What, the mother and daughter?" I had seen them, the daughter going off to school in a green gingham dress, with a folder covered in pink heart-shaped stickers. "Are you sure?"

"There's no other kids here apart from Jessica."

"It's definitely not her. She grizzles but doesn't scream."

We listened again.

"Do you think we should go up there?" I asked.

The Traffic Warden shook his head. "I don't know if it's a good idea to poke your nose into other people's business."

"I know, but what if the child's in danger?"

"The hallway's probably making it sound worse than it is."

"Do you really think?"

"Yeah. She's just throwing a tantrum, and it's bloody

inconsiderate of them to put her out so we all have to hear it, if you ask me."

"She's about ten."

"So?"

"Too old for tantrums. And what if the mother's not there, and it's a babysitter or something? She might not know."

"I've never seen anyone else going up there." He started walking away, towards the sitting room. "Leave it. Not our place to investigate."

"And what if it was our child? Whose place would it be to investigate then?"

"Give it a rest." He sat on the sofa.

I followed him and stood in the doorway. "If I saw a story in the paper next week that something happened up there I'd never forgive myself."

"Why are you being so dramatic about it?"

"Why are you being so offhand about it? She might be in real pain up there and you won't even acknowledge the possibility."

"Well, go on up, then. I'm not stopping you."

But I didn't. I sat in the hallway, listening and waiting, until all went quiet.

"Let's get a takeaway," the Traffic Warden said.

I was still sitting on the hallway floor, thinking. I heard him but didn't answer.

He crouched next to me. "Belly loves curry."

I didn't smile. "If you want."

He put his lips on my head and spoke into my hair. "Come on, Belly, cheer up."

I pushed him off his haunches, and we wrestled on the floor until he had me totally pinned.

*

It wasn't until Kim actually arrived that I realised I'd been waiting for her.

I was doing the post by the door, so I got first look.

The baby was beautiful. She was sleeping, tiny fists and a pink fleece hat, and I felt a small ache, like a little part of me melting. I wanted to say something, but I didn't know what, so I just said, "How're the sleepless nights?"

"Oh my God, it's a nightmare! She's a little madam, she really is."

I'd have expected myself to be relieved that she wasn't a gushing mother, but I wasn't.

Thankfully Mary came over and so did Ruth, and both being mothers they asked good questions so I didn't have to speak.

The baby woke up. She didn't cry, but peered around the office.

"Do you think you'll come back to work?" Ruth asked.

"Oh, as soon as possible. She's really not making me happy at all."

Mary started speaking to the baby, and the baby watched her, totally entranced. "Haven't you got lovely eyes?" Mary said. "Haven't you got the eyes of an old soul?"

I texted Rachel when I got back to my desk. I told her that I missed her and if she wanted to chat or anything to let me know.

There was no reply.

When I went down the office stairs to go home, I saw my body falling in front of me, my limbs splayed awkwardly and bloodied at the bottom. I had seen myself dragged onto the train tracks every day for so long that the visions hardly disturbed me at all, no matter how macabre. They weren't the worst thing that could happen. Death wasn't the thing that filled me with most dread. On the way back home I walked under the sign.

That evening the white noise I had heard in the flat seemed slightly louder, so I wondered if it was some appliance or something in the flat and I went looking.

I went to the kitchen first, but I couldn't hear anything over the fridge motor. There was nothing in the bedroom. I looked in the airing cupboard, but the boiler was silent.

I stood totally still, listening for the source, but it couldn't be found.

The second kitchen bulb cracked and died. The light was one of those fancy stainless steel fixtures and had three bulbs, and although the first had gone some time ago I hadn't done anything about it because there were two others.

Now the lone remaining bulb produced a sort of spotlight effect over the work surface. I was about to change the dead two, I had my hand on the handle of the cupboard under the sink, but I decided to do an experiment and see how long it took the Traffic Warden to do something about it.

That night I dreamt that I had a baby of my own.

It was a quick dream, and a happy one, which was peculiar. I just kept looking at him through the bars of a cot, sleeping on his belly in his blue baby grow. I was so pleased to have him, so content to be near him.

I thought about the dream on the train the next day.

When I was about ten, my mum told me I'd been born with all the eggs I'd ever have and I was totally stunned. I wondered if that was why I was feeling something that the Traffic Warden didn't: that

I loved my son as if he was already with me, like a huge reserve not waiting to be created but just waiting to be discovered.

Then I wondered if I only felt this way because it was so easy, because it was expected that the love a woman had for her child was ultimate and unsurpassed, and I could have as many ideas as I liked about the way things would be; I had no evidence for any of it.

I could imagine holding my baby up in the air, showing him to the world and showing the world to him, a new magic brought to everything because of him.

Or I could imagine piles of washing and all the shit and vomit and getting up in the night while the Traffic Warden slept.

Nothing was guaranteed.

*

"So. What do you want to do for your birthday?"

He was playing *Halo*, but I wasn't invited to join after last time when I kept dying. "I don't really care," he said.

"It's only a few weeks away. We could have a few mates over for drinks. Or go out in Brighton. Or we could have your parents over for dinner or something. I don't mind cooking. Hey, we could have a fondue if you like."

"Do whatever you want."

"It's your twenty-fifth birthday."

"I really just don't care." He sort of sniggered, and I felt my hackles rise.

"How can you be so indifferent to everything around you?" I phrased it like a question but it wasn't and we both knew it.

He didn't look up. "Oh, don't start going on again."

I started walking away, though I wasn't going anywhere. "Going on. Going on." I mumbled it so he could hear. "I'm starting to think we'll be going on like this forever."

"Well, you're the one starting all the arguments."

I was in the kitchen doorway when I turned back. "Well, excuse me for giving a fucking shit."

His look was open-mouthed and frowning. "Oh, give it up."

I threw a glass onto the kitchen floor, and the bits skittered across the tiles to the filth at the kickboard.

"What the fuck are you doing?"

I grabbed a pot plant that his mum had given us, raised it above my head and smashed that too. Soil sprayed outwards in a great dark star.

He put his Xbox controller down and got up.

"Oh, so you *can* put that thing down, then, once in a while. That's good to know."

"What the fuck is this about?"

"What the fuck is *anything* about? What the fuck is your job about, and what the fuck is your life about?"

"Have you gone mental?"

"Yeah, maybe I have. You can't just bow out of every decision there is, you know. You can't just be indifferent about *everything*. You used to be so passionate. Where has it all gone? Don't you give a shit about *anything* any more?"

He said nothing, which just made me more furious. I wanted him to shout at me so much.

"Look at us! I can't bear to raise kids who have a father who doesn't give a shit about anything."

"Why can't you just trust me to find my own way?"

"Why? Why? Because we've been living together for almost a year and you haven't moved a fucking muscle, that's why. I mean, what, did you dream of being a traffic warden? Is that all you are? Did you dream of living in this place? How can I trust you when we aren't moving anywhere? Answer me that."

190

"I can't help it if I don't know what I want."

"And your solution is what? Sitting on that fucking sofa, waiting for something to fly in the window? It's not exactly the most inspiring model for life. Don't you ever wonder why I'm thinking about the future of my children, when you can't even think about the future of your*self*?" I put my face in my hands and then pulled my nails across my cheeks. "I refuse, I absolutely refuse to *drag* you through life, arranging it all around you like you're some prince and I'm just a sort of peripheral figure, forcing you into having a marriage and having children and having a house and having a birthday, handing you your whole life on a fucking platter."

His whole face had darkened. I thought I'd never seen him so angry and I was glad.

"Yeah, yeah, sure, I mean I just can't *wait* to get you under my thumb and crush you down to nothing."

"Oh, *fuck* you. This is not just about *me*."

"Well, I'm happy as I am. If you're not, maybe it's time to call it a day."

"Yeah, sure, a great solution. Relationship not going well? Just jack it in. Because who gives a *fuck*?"

He started shouting back but I felt his grip on my upper arm and lost what he was saying as I tugged it away. "Don't you *dare* grab me, don't you fucking dare—"

"I'm *not*, I just—" But we both knew he had and he punched the lounge door next to my head, so hard that it flew back and hit the wall with a crack.

To my own surprise, I didn't shrink back, but stepped closer. "Come on then, you fucking arsehole, hit me."

"Oh, fuck off." He started for the bedroom to get his coat.

I wanted to launch the worst obscenities that I could think of, but I knew they wouldn't be true or make things right. I had been with enough arseholes to know he wasn't one.

There was no name for him.

"Don't walk away. Let's finish this."

He didn't stop, but stormed past me and slammed the front door.

I went to the bathroom and sat on the edge of the bath for a long minute. I wondered if I was making all the problems for myself. And for him.

I paced up and down like a caged animal, feeling the silence and emptiness of the flat. My dad always said there were different blacks, blue-black, purple-black, red-black. There are degrees of silence and emptiness too.

I went and looked at the living-room door. It was solid but he'd made quite a dent in it, and I put my fingertips in the hole. I wondered if I was ripping us apart from the inside.

I looked at the Venus fly trap on the windowsill. One of the mouths had an insect husk in it, and I used the tweezers to carefully pull it out. Sad little carcass. Then I swept up the glass and soil from the kitchen floor.

When he came back he smelt of smoke.

"I'm sorry," I said. I was standing by the hole in the door, and folded my arms.

"So am I."

One of us put the kettle on, and I was cold so I wrapped a blanket around my shoulders and sat on the sofa with the tea like someone in a film after some horrific experience. "Well, clearly, we love each other," I said.

He sat beside me. "Clearly."

"But what if love isn't enough?"

"Isn't enough for what?"

"I don't know. Life. Us. *Something.*" I tucked a clump of hair behind my ear, but it was already tucked. "Do you ever feel like we're living two entirely separate lives, but they just happen to be alongside each other? Like two parallel lines that never meet."

"No."

"Well, I do. I want us to be more than the sum of our parts."

"Do you want to get married?"

I watched a little group of bubbles swirling around on the top of my tea. "Do you remember how we were at uni?" He didn't say anything, and I felt like some old lady who couldn't let go of the past. "You seemed so *different* from everyone else. From anyone I'd ever known. I felt like you were made for me. I used to imagine, what if I hadn't gone to that uni and we hadn't met, and it's almost unthinkable." I took a sip of hot tea and felt it sliding inside me. "I'm ashamed to admit it, but I thought you were going to save me."

His voice was quiet. "Save you from what?"

"Oh, you know, from… being a Stepford wife. A wanker on the tube. Maybe just from being like everybody else. I don't know, I just… I don't want to be someone who gets in from work and sits in front of the telly. I don't want to be a run-down mum. I don't want to wake up one day and realise that I can't remember what DVD I watched the night before, and I've had the same takeaway every Friday night for the last however-many years. I don't want to waste my life, but I don't know how to spend it well. I feel like I have to do something *now* and if I don't, I'm going to hate myself —"

"You know what I think?"

"You do have thoughts in that head, then?"

He smiled. "Once in a blue moon. I think – maybe you

romanticised your idea of me a bit. When we first met, I mean."

I put my tea on the coffee table and rested my head on his chest. It felt warm and hard. "It's possible. Perhaps I mistook your indifference for some sort of wisdom." My voice sounded muffled against his sweatshirt. "I just wish I was brave enough to forget about what's expected of me."

He kissed me on the temple. "You are."

I said nothing.

We held each other tightly.

I squeezed him hard, as if he was going to pop. He laughed.

*

For some time, agreements had been coming in bigger chunks, and the pile was now taller than Rachel's filing.

"Shaun, are you gonna talk all day?"

"That's really funny because—"

"It was a rhetorical question."

"What's that?"

"It's a question that you don't need to answer. It was like a hint. A way of me saying, please, *please* get on with some work. We've got enough agreements to get through."

"What are you gonna do if I don't?"

"I'll—" I looked around. "I'll stab your Arsenal bear through the head. He'll never see the light of day again."

I knew instantly it was a mistake to joke with Shaun as he just saw it as a way to talk more, but it was too late. He grabbed the squashy pink pig off my monitor, the one Mel left behind, and held his pen above it, as if holding it to ransom.

At that moment, Big Nathan appeared silently behind him.

Afterwards I thought I should have acknowledged him so that Shaun would have known he was there, but I didn't do anything, and Big Nathan and I watched Shaun stab the pig repeatedly with his pen. Even Ruth stopped typing and swivelled round to watch.

Shaun only realised there was someone behind him when he pushed his chair back to get more leverage over the pig and hit Big Nathan's shiny black shoe.

He peered upwards and visibly shrank.

"Can I have a chat with you for a minute, Shaun?"

"Yeah."

And he followed Big Nathan out and down to the office downstairs, where I'd had my interview.

I exchanged looks with Ruth.

"Well, that was long overdue," she said. But she didn't comment further and nor did I.

When Shaun slunk back in, he sat down without a word, gave me the mangled pig back and was quiet for the whole afternoon.

Ian came round with an envelope of paper slips. "Sweepstake?"

"Oh, yeah, it's the Grand National this weekend, isn't it?"

"Certainly is."

I dug about in my purse for the money, and put my hand in the envelope. "I feel sorry for the horses I pick."

"Why?"

"Because I definitely won't win."

"Hey, you never know."

"No, trust me, this one I do know." My two horses had French names that I couldn't say.

"Still no Rachel?" he asked.

I pulled a sad face. "Nope."

"You miss her?"

"Yeah."

I watched as Kelly picked her horses.

"What did you get?" I asked, when Ian had moved on to Kyle.

"*Comply or Die* and *Simon*."

"Aw, there's a horse called Simon? Those names are much better than mine."

She shrugged and left her slips on the desk. "I don't even know what a sweepstake is."

When I went over to do submission, Mary was spreading cream cheese on a rice cake.

"Hungry?" I asked.

She finished a mouthful. "I missed lunch."

"What, working?"

"No, I had to go up the town, get the shopping. My boys, I tell you, they eat just as much as when they were teenagers."

I was waiting for MRP to load. "How old are they, then?"

"Twenty-six and twenty-eight."

"And they still live at home?"

"Yeah. They like having their meals cooked for them, I think."

"You're a big softie." I wrote the MRP numbers down in the column. "Don't they want to leave, though? I mean, as soon as I turned eighteen, I was itching to get out."

"Boys are different, I think."

"Are they?"

"I have to make four different dinners each night to keep everyone happy."

"Seriously?"

She nodded.

"That's a lot of work," I said. "I think I'd just tell them to like it or lump it."

"Does your bloke do his own washing and stuff, then?"

"He certainly does. He has an infuriating way of hanging it all around the flat, but I don't see why I should go poking round in his dirty clothes." I wrote my submission guesses down and saw Young Nathan write his.

"You wanna hang on to that one," Mary said.

"Why? Because he's capable of loading the washing machine?"

"Don't underestimate it, I tell you. You're lucky."

"Ooh, I feel so liberated."

"Have you heard from Rachel?" She finished the rice cake and started peeling an orange.

"No, I haven't. Has anyone in the office?"

She shook her head.

"I wonder if I should go and see her and make sure she's okay, but I don't want to invade her privacy. What do you think?"

"Well…" She raised her eyebrows pointedly and handed me a segment of orange. "Some people never ask for help, even when they need it the most."

*

I started to play a new game on the way back from work.

I'd be walking along and just close my eyes and keep walking, counting my steps to see how many I could do. I found that I could only take a few steps before I became unsure of the concrete under my own shoes, and no matter how many times I tried, I never made it over fifteen steps.

When I got home, I heard a familiar bassline from upstairs. The Traffic Warden was in the deckchair, but there was no sunset to see as the sky was still thick with cloud. He was smoking.

"How many tickets did you give out?"

"One."

"Did you ever go to the doctor?"

"About what?"

"About the disease that was sure to be threatening your life. Prostate cancer or whatever it was."

"No. I'm still thinking about it."

"Oh, right." Part of me wished I hadn't reminded him.

"But I can't think at the moment, because of that fucking cunt upstairs."

I started peeling my uniform off.

"Doesn't Dusty have a life? I mean, the guy's about forty, and *this* is how he chooses to spend his time. Does he even have a job? Fucking sad act. Fucking CUNT!"

I said nothing.

"I think we're living in the noisiest place in the universe, I really do. If we haven't got brats screaming their heads off, it's dickheads playing their music, and arseholes mowing their fucking lawns."

I smiled. He was right about the lawn thing. I hadn't known a dry weekend yet where I couldn't hear a mower or strimmer somewhere. "Well, Toto, we're deep in suburbia now. Why don't you just go up there and ask them to turn it down?"

"Five more minutes, and I will."

He lit another cigarette, but showed no signs of movement. I finished getting changed and made for the kitchen.

"All of their mates are cunts, too."

"Who?"

"Upstairs."

"Oh."

"You can tell just by looking at them. You see someone in the car park, you think, *they look like a cunt*, and sure enough, off they go upstairs."

"I really can't understand why you don't just go up there. Maybe they don't know, maybe they think we don't mind. Just tell them, and take it from there."

"Come with me, then."

"No, I don't want to."

"Go on, I need you."

"Me? What do you need me for? It's got nothing to do with me."

The doorbell went and I opened the door.

"Oh, hello, Mike," I said. "How are you?"

He looked straight over my shoulder at the Traffic Warden, who was coming down the hall behind me. "Can you hear that?"

I felt mischievous, so I answered him. "Yes. Loud, isn't it? Have you asked them to turn it down?"

Still he spoke to the Traffic Warden. "No, I haven't, but I will. I've got very sensitive hearing, you know. I can hear the crossing beeping at the end of the road there, I can."

"What? The crossing outside the station? That's about half a mile away."

"I can hear it, I can."

I knew it couldn't be true but I wasn't going to argue with him.

"Is it flat ten?" he went on. "I always smell curry coming out of there."

I was trying too hard not to laugh, so the Traffic Warden had to answer. "No, it's number nine, above us, I think, Mike."

"Are you going up?"

"I might, if it goes on much longer."

"Very inconsiderate. I've got very sensitive hearing."

I couldn't hold my laughter in any longer, so I stepped out from between them and went to the kitchen to start the dinner, but leaned over the counter laughing silently.

Five minutes later I heard the door shut and the Traffic Warden came in. "What a fucking *nutcase*."

"He's a crackpot, all right."

"Yeah, what the hell was the curry thing all about? The only flat that smells like curry is ours."

I started chopping an onion. "Fuck knows. There's no way he can hear those lights beeping, either. Your hearing peaks at sixteen and then it's all downhill. If it was true, he'd be able to hear a fly buzzing in here. He'd be driven crazy with noise! He'd have been up every five minutes telling us to be quiet."

"Perhaps you scared him off."

"Yeah, he's not a fan of mine, is he? What's that all about?"

"He knows you're a bint."

"Yeah, well, if it wasn't for me, you'd be just like him." I slid the onion into the melted butter in the frying pan. "What a strange life the man has."

"How do you mean?"

"Well, what pleasure can he get out of life? He's just passing the days until death."

"Aren't we all?"

The music from upstairs suddenly stopped.

We waited.

"Oh, the blissful silence." The Traffic Warden opened the fridge and stared inside at the food glowing yellow.

"Oi, I'm making dinner here."

"I can see that."

"Hey, you know what I found out today? This woman at work, Mary, still has her sons living at home, and they're like twenty-six and twenty-eight or something. *And* she makes four different dinners every night. One for her, one for her husband, and one each for her sons."

"Fucking mental." He took out the block of cheese and started eating it straight from the pack. I handed him a knife and he started cutting slices off.

"It *is*. It is fucking mental. They've lived there for far too long anyway, and they can't even be bothered to cook for themselves."

"She probably won't let them."

"Yeah, but no one had to *let* me. I just did it." I stirred the pasta to feel it all separating around my spoon. "Give us a bit of cheese."

He cut me off a slice and I ate it off the knife. "Yum."

He finished with the cheese and put it away.

"Do you think I should go and see Rachel?" I asked.

"You still haven't heard from her?"

"Not a sausage."

"Maybe give it until the end of the week."

"Hmmm."

*

The next day, Shaun got his inputting record. Young Nathan showed him how to look up the inputting numbers on the system, so he told me our scores at ten o'clock and eleven, and then at twelve I saw his eyes flit to his phone and then stare intently into the screen as if it had the answers to everything.

"I don't want to hear it," I said.

And he didn't say it.

At 15.01, he told me he'd beaten his record.

"That's great," I said. "Your medal's in the post."

"Yeah, you know what, though? I think I should get a bonus."

I felt like speaking my mind, so I did. "What, because you've finally started doing your job?" I felt no remorse, as I would have a year ago. The older I got, the less I felt like being nice for the sake of it.

Kelly won the sweepstake.

When I got home I got changed and did last night's washing-up.

The Traffic Warden was late.

I imagined my foot slipping on the kitchen floor and my skull smashing on the sideboard. I imagined him coming home and finding me dead in the kitchen, blood sliding out from underneath my body, in a dark and silky pool.

*

On Thursday I went to Londis at lunchtime to get some sweets, and I was served by Bobby. He had the patch of dribble on his chest like usual.

"Hello," I said.

"Hello, Madam."

"You all right?"

"Yes, thank you, Madam." He beeped my humbugs through. "Ninety-nine pee, please, Madam."

I gave him a pound. "Thanks."

"Thank you, Madam, thank you." He opened the till drawer and thought for a minute and then gave me one penny.

"Thanks."

"Thank you, Madam, thank you very much."

At submission I took the sweets over. "Humbug, anyone?"

"Ooh, humbugs. Where did these come from?" Young Nathan asked.

"Somewhere very exotic: Londis down the road."

Ian was on the phone but wedged it under his shoulder and put his hands together like he was going to catch something, so I threw one at him and he gave me a thumbs-up.

I held out the packet to Mary and she shook her head. "You weren't served by that Bobby, were you?"

"Yes, but I don't think it sullied the sweets."

Mary wrinkled her nose. "He makes me feel sick."

"Sick? Why?"

"I went to school with him," Young Nathan said, taking a humbug.

"Did you?"

"Yeah. He's a few years older than us. You know he's not really like that, don't you?"

"What do you mean? He's not disabled?"

"Not one bit. He's putting it on. We used to work in the deli together in Tesco and sometimes he'd serve customers with his" – he mouthed *cock* – "hanging out and stuff like that."

I laughed. "Oh my God, you are kidding me."

"No."

"Are you serious?"

"Yeah."

I took a sweet myself, choosing one with thicker dark stripes as they seemed chewier for some reason. "He's not putting it on. He can't be."

"He is."

"What on earth would make somebody do that? Do you have any idea?"

He pushed his glasses up his nose and drained the last of his squash from his *Brave New World* mug. "I really don't know."

When I got back to my desk, Ruth had her head in her hands. I wished Rachel were there, because she'd have known what to say.

"Are you all right?" I asked her.

Ruth looked up. "Well, no, since you ask. I'm totally swamped."

"Is there anything I can help with?"

"Put more hours in the day?"

There was an awkward silence.

"Thanks for asking, but there's not much. I've got three days' worth of emails, the post to check, cheques to go on the system, the stage fours to print, these to go in the post..." She held up a large chunk of papers.

"I can take those. And the stage fours," I said.

"I couldn't ask you to do that. You've got enough on your plate." The agreements were starting to build up, and Shaun had slipped back into his old habits.

"It's fine. Really."

"Well, thanks." She handed me the stack and I went over to sort them out. As I looked over the post holes, I found quite a few that I wasn't familiar with.

One was labelled *RTW*. RTW... I knew that from somewhere, but I couldn't think where. There was another underneath it that said *FREEMANS – NO MORE, HAND TO NDW*, but I had no papers for that one, so luckily I didn't have to work out who or what NDW was.

*

By Friday I'd still heard nothing from Rachel, and so after work I walked down to Sainsbury's and bought a few provisions, and then I walked to her flat.

A small blonde girl with Rachel's cheekbones opened the door.

"Hello," I said. "Amy?"

She didn't say anything but nodded. She had pyjamas on, sky blue and dotted with little penguins.

I told her my name and then said, "I'm here to see your mum."

She stepped away from the door and I went in. I felt like a

burglar.

"She's in bed." She said it so quietly I could barely hear her, and stood wobbling, one foot over the other, in a sitting room strewn with toys.

"Is she asleep?"

She looked at the floor and said nothing.

I remembered which one was her bedroom from the time I had been there before, and knocked softly on the door.

There was no response.

I knocked louder.

Rachel's voice. "What do you want?"

"I want to check you're okay. Can I come in?"

"Oh, God, it's you."

"Oh, God, it's me." There was a pause. "So can I come in, then?"

"No."

"Sadly you don't have much choice." I opened the door. The curtains were drawn and I could barely see anything in the dusty gloom. The air was heavy with the smell of sleep and sadness. There were empty or half-empty drinks around her bed and bedside table, but no plates, so she obviously hadn't eaten anything for a while. She sat up, and her hair stuck out on her head like a dishevelled bird. She looked miserable.

"I look like such a fucking state."

"What's new?"

She didn't smile.

"I'm going to open the curtains," I said, and put my shopping bag on the bed while I picked my way over to the window. "I've brought you some food."

"I don't feel like eating."

"Well, I'm not leaving until you've had something, so have a look."

I unlocked the window and opened it to let some air in, and I heard the plastic bag rustle.

"Smoked salmon."

"Yeah."

"And jelly beans. Amy will be your best mate."

"Yeah, I met her. She looks like you."

"I know." She sank back on the pillows.

I sat on the bed. "I was sorry to hear about your dad. I didn't even realise he was ill or anything."

"Yeah, it's why we moved back down here. One of the reasons." She played with a soggy tissue in her hands. "Sorry I went off without saying anything. I just couldn't—" She stopped. "You know."

"Yeah. Sort of."

Neither of us said anything.

"This isn't like you, though," I said. "Is it? What about Amy? She needs you."

"I know she fucking does."

She started crying, and I searched around for some more tissues and found a bog roll by the bed, which I gave her.

"I'm sorry, I'm so sorry..."

"Don't worry about it," I said. "Sorry. I didn't come here to lecture you."

There was a pause, and she kept crying. I wasn't sure I was doing much good.

"You can cry for as long as you like. We can chat for as long as you like. But just so you know," I said, "I'm not leaving here until you've had a shower, and eaten something, and let me put a load of washing on."

She stared out the window at the clouds, looking completely vacant. "I'm so… embarrassed."

"Don't be silly. What for?"

"Seeing me like this…" She waved a limp hand over her face and let it drop to the bed again.

"I don't give a shit." I remembered. "Sorry, I forgot about Amy."

"Don't worry, she… she knows all the swear words."

"I wonder who she picked those up from."

"Hmmm."

"How about getting in the shower now? Have a wash and put some clean clothes on. Yeah?"

She still looked vacant.

"Rachel?"

"Okay, okay."

"Do you want me to help you, or are you going to be all right?"

"I'll be all right. Oh, God. I'm so sorry. And thanks. For coming."

As soon as she went into the bathroom, I started picking up the clothes from the floor and stripped the bed down. I gathered up all the old tissues and threw them away, and carried the cups to the kitchen. I was choosing a programme on the washing machine in the kitchen when I realised Amy was watching me from the doorway.

"Hey," I said to her. "How are you?"

She didn't answer, but just swung off the door handle. I was always a bit uncomfortable around kids that I didn't know well, and often felt that, like primeval beasts, they could smell my fear. It was nothing sinister; it was just that I could never tell how much they understood. I used to hate being patronised, so as an adult I tried to speak to them like adults, but more often than not they didn't seem to have a clue what I was on about.

"Want some jelly beans?" I asked.

She stopped swinging and nodded.

We were talking when Rachel came out of the bathroom. She was wearing a vest top and clean pyjama trousers, but her hair was wet and unbrushed.

"Amy, where's your mum's hairbrush?"

Rachel touched her head. "Oh…"

Amy went off to get it.

"Cup of tea?"

Rachel shook her head and some water drops fell on the floor.

Amy came back with the brush and knelt behind her mum on the sofa.

"So how's work?" Rachel asked. "I need to talk about something other than – you know. Tell me all the juicy gossip."

"Well, it's Weblands, so there's really nothing juicy to tell." But I told her about Bobby the fake, about Kim's baby, about Mary's sons, about Shaun stabbing the pig.

I waited until Amy had brushed her hair smooth and they were having a cuddle, and then opened the smoked salmon. I peeled a slice, folded it and put it into my mouth, and then left the packet on the sofa next to Rachel. "That is really good, you know. Amy, you want some fish?"

She shook her head.

I rubbed my stomach. "Oh, you're missing out. It's so *yummy*. It's *so* good."

Rachel sighed. "You won't let up on this, will you?"

I shook my head, my mouth still full. "Absolutely not."

She took a small piece and ate it, chewing soberly.

"I do have an ulterior motive, though," I said. "And it's very selfish."

"Really? What?"

"I'm going totally bananas without you at work."

She almost smiled. "You've got Young Nathan. And Ian."

"True. But I have to sit opposite Shaun. And lately I've been wondering why, as if maybe I did something awful in a past life, or something."

"No luck at the interview, then?"

"No. Guy turned out to be a bit of an a-hole."

"What's a a-hole?" Amy asked, and it sounded so funny coming out of her sweet pink mouth and as soon as I caught Rachel's eye, neither of us could help laughing.

*

On Sunday morning, I was reading and waiting for the Traffic Warden to come back from the shop.

I was three quarters of the way through a novel about an office, and the whole thing was told from the perspective of "we", like "we felt such and such on Monday mornings" and "we thought such and such about our boss". At first, I found it slightly wearing, because I was waiting for the narrator to let up and speak normally. I thought he was trying to make a point about distant managers who never consider their workers individuals.

But then the book went the other way and I thought how nice, how life-affirming it was for that narrator to feel that he was part of one homogenous lump, to know the same things and speak the same jargon that every workplace did. The work was a way of being accepted in a group. Had I always felt alone in Weblands? At least until Rachel had come and even then, sometimes. I couldn't understand what anyone else was doing there. There really was no "we".

Yet no one else in the office had any reason to look at me and think I was different. I showed up at nine every day, did my work, and left at five as if this was all my existence meant, when nothing terrified me more. Perhaps they were all terrified too.

I heard the Traffic Warden's key in the door, and he came into the bedroom with a snapped-in-half baguette under his arm.

"You know, I really think socks and sandals are a great combination."

I held out my hand and he broke off a hunk of bread, showering the duvet in crumbs.

"You look fucking ridiculous."

"Guess what?" He chewed on a bit of bread. "Upstairs car tax has run out. I'm going to report it to the DVLA."

"God, you must've been *gleeful* when you saw that."

"No, I was infuriated." We both paused, chewing. He was staring out the window at something, even adjusting the blinds to get a better look. "Cunts."

*

On Monday morning I woke up at five thirty, in the middle of a dream about an old lover.

He had not treated me well and all I remembered from my dream was him looking at me like I was dirt, a familiar expression on his pale features.

It had been a peculiar relationship in that I had fluctuated between doing anything he wanted and being sure that he was the devil incarnate. He said that our love was a miracle because it was based on an animal instinct that couldn't be resisted. He said that it was meant to be and we were just pure creatures, following our destiny. Even though I didn't believe a word, the notion seemed so

210

romantic that I almost didn't notice that our relationship was based mainly on shagging in the stock room.

The dream had caused me to knock the wall behind our bed and it was that that made me felt guilty. I wondered if I had moaned his name in the early and silent hours, but if the Traffic Warden heard me he didn't say anything about it.

At seven, I got up and showered, and then I ate my cereal in the kitchen doorway, watching the Traffic Warden on the sofa. He had bought a bottle of squeezy honey, and sat in front of *BBC Breakfast*, oozing blobs onto his palm and licking them off.

When I got to work I noticed that Shaun hadn't been finishing the filing that I'd been giving him each day when I did submission, so he had a disordered, two-inch wedge of build-up in his in-tray. I'd wondered why Ruth and Ian kept asking me if I'd seen certain transmittal forms.

"Filing's building up a bit," I commented, pretending I had only just seen it. I didn't like having to force his hand, but I couldn't see why I should do everything just because he didn't want to. It wasn't how a job should work.

Shaun was unresponsive, but I wasn't going to let it drop.

"We had an agreement. You file, I do the post."

"I'll do it tomorrow."

I knew he was lying. "Okay."

*

I forgot to watch him the next day when I went to do submission.

Instead I asked Young Nathan how the novel was going.

"All right. About three quarters through by now, so it's starting to come together."

Mary's ears pricked up. "What's it about?"

Young Nathan seemed unabashed. "It's about working here, actually."

"What, this office?"

"Yeah."

"Oh, God, how boring."

"I don't think it is," Young Nathan said. "I don't want to go through life without finding anything interesting enough to record."

"Are we in it?" Mary asked.

"Sort of."

She wrinkled her nose in disgust.

"And how's *Nana*?" I asked.

"*Nana*'s fine, thanks."

"Have you abandoned it yet?"

"No."

"Really? Or is it just that you don't want to admit it?" I wrote my submission guesses down, and saw that Young Nathan was doing the same.

"I haven't, though."

"What, you're seriously going to finish it? I don't believe you."

"Don't doubt me, sister."

"If you say so, savage."

MRP had just finished, so I started loading ICS. "There's a problem with the submission game. I was thinking about it earlier."

"What?"

"Well, with the graph in the equation there's never going to be a winner. We could just keep going forever, never being any the wiser."

"Let's put a date on it, then." He opened his drawer, took out a

212

shiny red apple and bit into it.

"What about our performance reviews? Those'll be in April sometime."

"A month away."

"Yeah. That's okay, isn't it?"

"We don't know when they're coming, though," he said.

"The last day in April, then."

"Agreed."

"Am I in the lead?"

"You might be."

For some weeks I had been sitting right down the platform, on a wind-beaten bench where I had never had company. As a result, it had been a while since I'd seen Reading Woman, or Helmet Man, so I decided to sit in my old place and wait for them, see if they still came.

They came.

They looked the same. I wondered if they'd be surprised to see me, but they didn't appear to notice me. Reading Woman had her book out straight away, and Helmet Man had his hands in his pockets, scuffing back and forth on the platform.

I looked for Henri Lloyd but he was nowhere to be seen, so I took my own book out. The one about the office. I looked at the words for some time, but I couldn't read.

As soon as I got in, I changed my clothes and I went to give blood.

I had to wait an hour before I was called behind a screen by a grey-haired nurse who didn't meet my eye.

She didn't warn me before she stuck a little plastic pin in my finger, and I watched a drop get sucked into a little pipette. Then she squeezed it into an open test tube of turquoise liquid. It made a bubble as it came out.

"What's that for?" I asked.

We both watched the drop of blood slowly sinking to the bottom, like we were watching some extraordinary creature in an aquarium.

"Iron." She smiled. "You're fine."

I went back to the plastic chairs to wait. I took my book out but still couldn't read it.

I looked around the hall. Behind me was a gurney where a woman with frizzy blonde hair was giving blood. She had a little girl of about ten with her.

"Are you worried about Mummy? Hold Mummy's hand."

I listened to her fussing the whole way through, telling the girl to close her eyes and not look at the blood.

I decided that when I had a child and I brought them with me, I'd say, *This doesn't hurt. There's nothing wrong with me. It's a perfectly normal thing to do.*

But whether you wanted to or not, you passed all your neuroses onto your children. Perhaps that was why people had children, so they could have a little clan of people who thought like they did. So we were all just recycled forms of what had gone before. A photocopy of a photocopy.

A friend of mine had a baby when she was eighteen and she said that it gave her life a direction and meaning that she hadn't had before. It didn't seem like a very good reason to have a baby.

When I was called, I lay on the blue leather gurney and watched the nurse labelling packets and tubs. She had a navy dress with white piping and flat black shoes, like every nurse I'd ever seen. Her name badge said *Julia*.

She flicked my skin, trying to get a vein, and brought out the needle, which was thicker than I remembered and cut diagonally at the end like a quill. I watched it sink into my skin. "You're brave," she said.

"How do you mean?"

"Most people don't like to watch it going in."

"My mum's a nurse," I said, as if it explained everything.

She rolled up a paper towel and taped it into a little cylinder. "Here," she said. "Roll that in your hand."

I felt compelled to make conversation, so I asked her if it was always this busy.

"Yeah, pretty much," she said.

"That's good."

The machine kept beeping, and when it did she would bend down and do something to make it stop. "There's nothing wrong, it's just coming out a bit slowly, drip by drip."

I looked around again, at the piles of bags, makeshift screens, collapsible bins, a fold-out table, and people waiting, shivering, lying on beds. A woman had her head in her hands on the refreshment table; another soberly chewed on biscuits. It was like a refugee camp or one of those films where there are only a few remaining humans and they gather in one room to wait it out, or decide how they're going to rebuild civilisation. How different would the world be if it was built by people who chose to give their own blood to help strangers?

"How long have you been doing this?" I asked.

"Three and a half years. Hoping to move on soon, though. There's got to be more to life than this."

When it was finished, I sat up and Julia pressed a blob of cotton wool to the inside of my elbow. Then she gave it to me to hold and I looked at the bag of blood as she scooped it from the machine beside us.

215

"It's so dark," I said.

"It's deoxygenated. If it wasn't, it'd be the colour of that bright red top."

I smiled. That was exactly what my mum would have said.

She held the bag for a moment, swilling it around in her hands like someone playing with a child's toy for the first time. She held it out. "Do you want to touch it?"

"No," I said, and then, "Actually, yeah."

She held it towards me, and I squeezed it.

"It's still warm."

"Yes."

I heated up a can of mushroom soup for dinner, and the Traffic Warden and I watched *How to Look Good Naked*. There was a girl on there who said that when she dressed up in high heels she felt like a transvestite, or a tractor dressed up in ribbons. I knew exactly what she meant.

She wore nothing but jeans and jumpers, until the presenter poofed her hair and dyed it blonde, and got her wearing pink lipstick and frilly knickers. I liked her at first but she looked more and more like she was really getting into it, and I grew bored.

I couldn't buy the idea of someone becoming a different person over the course of a programme. Even if it was possible, I couldn't see the need. There was a paradox there. If you could just become anyone you liked, then surely you weren't really anyone.

I'd thought she would buck the trend, and I realised that for a while I had been hoping that *someone* would do it. They could say, "Yeah, I see that the control pants make me look thinner, but I don't really care."

Just once.

But they never did.

The last kitchen bulb went. The Traffic Warden watched me set up a lamp on the surface. I felt both angry and cruel at once.

I sat on the edge of the bath to brush my teeth.

The Traffic Warden came and stood in the doorway. "Get out."

"I'm doing my teeth."

"I need a piss."

"I'm not stopping you."

"You know I don't like it when there's other people in the room."

"I was here first."

"Get out."

A recycled conversation. A photocopy of a photocopy.

We got into bed. The Traffic Warden forgot the spider check, but I wasn't about to warn him.

We read in silence for a while, me my book and him a magazine.

"Would you ever strip for a magazine shoot?" he asked.

I put my book down. "Depends."

"Well, you know, if you had a nice—" He stopped.

"Oh—"

"I mean, I love your body."

"Yeah, thanks, that means a lot."

"Come on, I'm always groping you."

"That doesn't mean you love me. I've been groped by plenty of people who don't."

"You know what I mean."

"Yeah, I think I'm hearing you loud and clear."

"Don't be silly, you know I didn't mean it."

"You know something? It's not even that I want you to think before you speak. I don't even want you to think those things about me. To have you, *you* tell me that I'm ugly is… well, I don't

217

even know what it is."

"I never said you were ugly."

"Sure."

"I know you don't really care about any of that shit, though. You're not like other women."

"I'm not, but... I thought you saw through all that, all that airbrushing and stuff."

"So I should lie to you, then? Is that it? Is that what you want?"

I saw red. "What I want, what I want, what a question! What a fucking question!" I put my book down and turned to him. "You know, you can't just say whatever the fuck you like under the guise of being honest. If I said whatever was on my mind we'd have a lot more arguments."

"Oh, why don't you just leave me, if I'm that bad?"

"That's not a way to end every argument."

"It is with the silly ones."

"Go fuck yourself."

I switched off the light and we lay with our backs to each other.

I thought of how we must look from above, like two angry prawns.

His voice in the dark. "What do you want from me?"

Was this the moment? I sighed. "I don't know."

The sheets rustled, and I felt his warm hand running down my side. I turned so I was lying on my back.

He stroked my hair. "You know I think you're beautiful."

But either I didn't believe him or it wasn't enough.

His fingers tugged at my knickers.

"You've got to be kidding."

"What?"

"I'm not just a hole that you can stick your dick in whenever you feel like it."

He moved away, and I heard him thump the sheet with his fist.

"Don't be like that," I said.

"Like what?"

"I don't know, this. It's crazy."

He turned back round. "Yes, it is crazy. *You're* crazy. You've read one too many books and it's turned you into some sort of neurotic feminist."

I opened my mouth and shut it again. I knew that those words would sit inside me forever, like a piece of shrapnel. There was a long silence. "Well, thank you, Brabantio."

"Who's Brabantio?"

"He's from *Othello* – Desdemona's father." I couldn't bear the silence between us and my words into the dark seemed to delay the inevitable. "She goes off to marry Othello and he discovers her missing in the night and says, 'How got she out?' and I remember our teacher saying what a genius Shakespeare was for that line, and I never understood what she meant but now I do." I shook my head. "*Now* I do. Because he could have said, 'How did she get out?' or any number of variations, but he didn't. He chose the one that makes it sound like she's a disobedient animal who should be brought back to him. Just like when you said, 'I'm not having you working'."

He sighed. "I knew that would come up again."

"Did you? Fucking *good*. Because I was angrier than I let on about that comment, but not as angry as I should have been. Not nearly enough."

I got up and started for the bathroom.

"Where are you going?"

"To burn my fucking bra."

I sat on the toilet and looked at my thighs, big and round and pale in the dark bathroom.

A few days before, I'd been getting out of the shower and I'd caught sight of my body in the mirror of our bathroom cabinet, just the mid-section, between shoulders and hips, like a headless sculpture.

I'd been surprised at how fertile I'd looked. I had run my hands over my sides, my rolling hips, my plump thighs. I could squeeze a big chunk of stomach.

I had suddenly thought, *I'm not nineteen any more*. I could conceive at any minute. I already looked like a mother.

I got back in bed and neither of us said anything. I bit my lip until I could taste blood. "We're in trouble."

More silence. Lights flashed across the ceiling. Then, "Are we?"

"Yeah."

"Why?"

"I don't know if I can – I don't know if I can do this any more."

"What?"

"Remember that time you said that you'd chosen what computer we were going to get when we 'settle down'… I don't know." I took a deep breath. "I feel as if we have a set choice of treadmills and we're just going to get on one and stay on it forever. I feel like I can see our lives together already, I can see me run ragged and you just playing on your Xbox in a spare room while I hoover around you, and I know I keep on at you about making something of yourself but the truth is I don't give a shit whether you're a traffic warden or the Dalai Lama, I don't want to hoover round anyone. I don't want to be any part of it."

I willed him to fight or to say the right thing, but I had no idea how either of those would be possible. "I know I've tried to change you, and I know that this is just who you are, and I don't hate you for it but I can't live with it either. I'm sorry. I have no idea what to do for the best, but it's not... *this*."

"Does all this stuff really matter to you, though?"

"Yeah."

"Really?"

"Yeah. Don't you understand? Can't you see it? If we don't *do* something we are going to *die* here."

"Come on, you're being dramatic."

"I knew you would say that. But I can't stay here. I won't. I can't."

"You can't get over this, can you?"

"No. Not while all the time I keep thinking, *Is this it? Is this all there's ever going to be?* Because I know this *is* it. I know this is it. And I don't even care if I'm the loneliest girl on the planet, I don't want *this* any more. What's the fucking point of being in a relationship if you still feel lonely?"

"But we're all alone."

"Being alone and being lonely are not the same thing."

"That's only your perspective."

"It is."

The space that had grown between us seemed cavernous.

He said nothing.

"Aren't you going to say anything?"

"Like what?"

Did I want him to tell me I was wrong? "Something."

"Well, I can't change who I am."

"No, I guess not." I ran my fingers through my hair. "We seemed so compatible."

"I know."

I sat up and sobbed in the dark. My hair went damp around

the edges, as if I had woken from a nightmare. "I'll never find anyone like you again."

"Oh, Belly." He sat up too, and hugged me, and I leaned against him. I could hear his words buzzing through his chest. "I don't think there's anything we can do."

I knew then that I was walking away and he was letting me go. I cried for a while and he held me. I could hear my tears plip on the duvet.

I took his hand where it was rubbing my arm and squeezed it as if it were the most precious thing in the world and he squeezed mine back. I ran my finger over his knuckles and held it up to my lips.

"If you want this so much, then why are you crying?"

I couldn't answer, so I just shook my head.

We swayed back and forth gently, without saying anything. I thought back, of all the people I had been good friends with, and I couldn't think of anyone who'd known me like he had.

"I love you."

"I love you, too."

*

He pulled out the sofa bed, and I brought a sheet and sleeping bag from the wardrobe.

"You don't have to be stuck here, you know," I said. "We can take it in turns, or swap after a month or something."

"It's fine."

I put the bedding on the other sofa. "I mean, I'm not the Queen of Sheba. You don't have to be uncomfortable. I don't—"

"Really. I don't mind."

"I don't want you to feel like you're being punished."

"I'll be fine. I've got the TV out here."

222

"And the Xbox, of course." I had to tell myself that it no longer had anything to do with me.

"Exactly. So I'll be fine."

"I don't hate you." I didn't know how to say goodnight and leave him; it wasn't in our repertoire of conversations. It was too polite and normal.

"I don't hate you, either."

"Okay."

"That's it, then."

"So… goodnight." And before he could answer I walked out, closing the door behind me.

*

The next night I got in from work and lay on the bed.

I wanted to think but I couldn't. I watched the sky.

I heard the door open and his socks on the carpet and I sat up and looked at him. His face seemed different already, a slightly warped representation of something very familiar.

"Do you want me to go?" he asked.

I fiddled with the pillow. We must have worn them in without noticing, because it didn't crackle any more.

"Did you hear me?"

"No." I was unable to meet his eye.

"I said —"

"I know. I know what you said. No, I don't want you to, particularly. It might be good for us, though. For now. It might be the best thing."

"Okay."

He walked out, leaving the door ajar.

After a while I went and stood in the lounge doorway, and

watched him scoop up his epaulettes from the table and coil his laptop wire and put the Xbox back in its packaging.

He saw me watching. "I told you the box would come in useful one day."

I went back into the bedroom and got into bed with all my work clothes still on.

His hand on my shoulder. "Bye, Belly," he said.

"Bye." I sat up and hugged him, but we took an awkward angle and my eye squashed against him. "Don't forget to eat your vegetables." It was a joke, but came out like I was nagging him.

"Will you be okay?"

"Yeah."

I lay back down and listened as he shut the bedroom door, and then the front door, and then as his footsteps faded down the corridor. I knew his engine noise, and like a faithful pet I listened to it fade away.

I noticed that evening that he hadn't even taken his toothbrush. A reminder of his presence, but not a promise of him coming back.

I felt like I'd been hollowed out. Suddenly fragile and sensitive.

An open mouth in a beehive.

Some nights I couldn't make dinner. I was totally incapable of thinking through a meal: the food groups, the jumbled cupboards, the shopping, the salt, the pans... something I had been doing for years seemed so complicated and impossible. And I didn't want to switch on that fucking lamp.

On those nights I just ate crisps until I wasn't hungry any more.

I watched TV, hours of it, without discrimination. Anything that was on. Old people watched less TV than me.

I couldn't remember anything else that I used to do.

I didn't want to do anything that I used to do.

Eventually all I had in the fridge was a jar of mayonnaise, so I went to the supermarket after work. I gave myself a temporary licence to stop worrying about money, like compassionate leave, so I didn't pick over a single product, or stand working out what was better value per kilogram than what, or what could be compromised on (noodles, cheese) and what couldn't (bread, fresh meat). Instead I just bought whatever looked good.

It occurred to me that if every product we bought together was a compromise, then neither of us had really ever been happy.

I bought smoked salmon, pistachio nuts, garlic cheese, fresh bread, chocolate cereal. I couldn't be sure whether I was cut adrift or free, but I felt like I was living well.

One day I went in and Rachel was sitting at her desk, a bit thinner, with thick kohl round her eyes, but otherwise the same.

I sat down next to her. "You're back."

"I'm back."

"How's it going?" I asked.

"Better. You know."

"Yeah. Well, I missed you."

"Only because your phone hasn't stopped ringing."

"Yeah. And your company."

Ruth piped up. She had a mouthful of apple. "I can vouch for her. At one point I had to give her my stapler to fix."

Rachel smiled.

We slipped back into an old routine. The office felt safe, like a sanctuary.

We did work, but I knew Ruth would go easy on us, so I

started a new game of putting the weird-sounding customers on speakerphone and mute, and doing impressions of them.

I was watching TV one evening when a wasp motored in. Once I would have yelped and run and got the Traffic Warden to kill it. It seemed completely pointless to even fuss when there was no one else there. I was still afraid, but I stood in the middle of the room, poised with a rolled-up paper, waited for it to land somewhere and then hit it until it was dead.

*

One afternoon, Big Nathan called me on the phone. I saw it was him but dropped my usual spiel, and just said, "Hello, Nathan."

"Oh, you know it's me."

I smiled. "Yes."

"Can you come over for a minute?"

"Of course."

Rachel was on the phone, so we just exchanged raised eyebrows and I went.

"Hello," he said.

I stood in front of his desk with my arms tucked behind my back, and went through in my mind what he could possibly have to tell me.

I was too miserable. It couldn't be tolerated any more; I didn't have a sunny enough disposition; my typing wasn't fast enough. My phone manner was bizarre and sad.

He swung his chair slightly so he faced me head-on, and put his hands together on the desk. "Shaun."

"Yes?"

"Has he done that filing?"

Ian or Ruth must have said something.

"No," I said. "He hasn't."

"How much is there, roughly?"

"Around a month's worth, maybe more."

He nodded, sagely. "Okay. Thank you."

"Okay."

I went upstairs to the toilets and when I came back, Shaun was in the hallway, talking on his mobile and leaning over the railing to look down the stairwell.

When I went back into the office, Big Nathan waved me over again.

"Just to let you know, I've let Shaun go."

"Right."

"Okay."

I felt like I should say something else. "Okay."

I went to my desk and sat down, and looked at the filing in Shaun's in-tray. I felt something between relief and guilt. Shaun came back. He didn't say anything.

"Big Nathan just told me," I said. "I'm sorry."

"It's all right," he said, and got his bag from underneath the desk. He put his Arsenal bear in, and then rinsed out his Arsenal mug and put that in too.

"You want a ciggie?" I asked. What a fraud I was.

"Yeah."

We walked out together and stood on the pavement outside, and I gave him a cigarette. "I was fired from my first job. If it's any consolation."

Shaun wasn't interested. "He said I'd get a decent last pay cheque."

I was sceptical but didn't comment. "Did he say why he was letting you go?"

"Not doing enough work."

"Really? Shaun, that is just shocking."

He smiled. "Yeah."

"Did he say anything else?"

"He said he hired me to liven up the office a bit, but I was talking too much."

"He actually told you the exact reason that he hired you?"

"Yeah. Why?"

"No reason. Well, good luck in your next job, whatever you end up doing."

We flicked our fag butts into the bushes simultaneously.

"Well, see ya."

"See ya."

That night there was a big storm.

I saw a white flash and the thunder cracked so loudly it sounded as if it was right above the flat. I opened the window and looked up and down the street; it was dark, and completely silent, and like something out of a film the rain started, slowly at first, and then as if someone was upending buckets.

I watched it rush in sheets down the middle of the road, and form channels down the gutter.

*

One Saturday morning I put his toothbrush on top of the bathroom cabinet.

Then I wiped all his hairs out of the shower.

Then I scrubbed every tile in the bathroom and washed every skirting board in the flat. I polished the windows, even getting rid of a blob of bird shit on the bedroom window with a broom. It had been bugging me since I'd moved in, and I would never have to look at it again.

I sorted out my clothes, pulling out everything I was too fat for and the five white shirts I'd bought when I'd first started at Weblands. I took them to the hospice shop in a bin liner, and bought three light bulbs.

When I got back home, I poured caustic soda down the plugholes, hoovered underneath the sofa cushions, descaled the kettle, and wiped the mould off the back of the front door.

I changed the kitchen bulbs and put the lamp back where it had come from.

At one point I started a list in my head called *Things I No Longer Have to Put Up With*. Number one. Washing hanging in the doorways. Number two. An excess of towels in the bathroom, or heaped on the bedroom floor, or worse, wet and on my side of the bed. Number three. The Duvet Thief.

I stopped the list.

*

The office was strange without Shaun. My workload was only marginally increased, but it felt silent. Also, I was back on twelve o'clock lunches permanently.

I hadn't bothered to make lunch, so I went into Londis to get a sandwich. Bobby was there; I hadn't seen him since Young Nathan had told me the truth about him. I watched him over the shelves. He was the same with every customer.

When he served me I looked at him carefully, to see if I could detect which bits of him were fake and which real.

"Thank you, Madam," he said, and he started to mechanically scan my stuff through the register. I could feel my mouth trying to

229

twist into a smile, but I didn't want to let on, in case people thought I was laughing for the wrong reasons.

He didn't have his name badge on, and I wondered if this was as deliberate as the dribble he'd put on his shirt.

"Thank you, Madam, thank you very much."

However much I wanted to say something, all I could do was look into his eyes and hope that he saw what I wanted him to see, that I *knew*. "Thanks, Bobby."

I went to the park as usual. The sky was a peculiar shade of yellow and slightly misty. It was warmer than it had been, though it was still stuffy, the air hanging thick as gauze. I noticed some bees sort of drunkenly bumbling their way around, but they didn't seem to have much purpose.

"What's it like out there?" Rachel asked, when I got back to my desk.

I sort of shrugged. "It's warm but not sunny. I don't know, really. Even the bees are confused."

She smiled.

"I know, because I asked them." I sat down, opened a bag of humbugs and offered them round customer services. As Ruth was handing them back to me, Big Nathan strode past.

"Aren't you going to offer me one?"

Something made me want to do another experiment. "Sorry – employee sweets only, I'm afraid. Maybe next time." My phone started ringing. "But, since my PR's coming up…" I picked up the receiver and passed him the bag. It was some customer quoting their reference number, so I put them on hold.

Big Nathan was still searching through the bag, so I motioned for the sweets back. "Hand them over, then. I've got a very busy reception to run here. I don't have time for messing about with sweeties."

He grinned and said nothing, but turned and went back across
the office with them.

Reception was quite busy that afternoon, but the calls had slowed
down a bit by three, so I went to do submission while I had the
chance.

Young Nathan looked smug. "Hey, how's it going?"

I started loading up MRP. "Oh, you know how it is." I wanted
to say something about the quietness since Shaun had gone, but
speaking ill of the fired was like speaking ill of the dead.
"Although *someone* stole my *humbugs*."

Big Nathan started laughing.

Mark, on the desk next to him, perked up above his monitor.
"Oh, yeah, thanks for the sweets, mate."

"Yeah, thanks for them," Ian said.

Mary swirled round on her chair. "Very *nice* of you."

I smiled, tight-lipped. "Any left?"

Young Nathan opened his drawer. "There might be one or
two…"

He pulled out the remainder of the bag and handed it over –
only one or two had even been taken.

"Oh, you absolute *scoundrels*."

Everyone was laughing.

"You really should know better than to come between me and
sugar."

Mary took out an orange and started peeling it. She swivelled in
her chair to face me. "Have you heard?"

I felt that my reaction was being watched carefully.

"Kim's coming back."

When I got home I was standing in the hallway, searching in my bag for my keys, when the screams started again from upstairs.

I heard the mother say, "If you don't behave, then you're not coming inside." The door clicked shut.

So the Traffic Warden was right. It had just been a child throwing tantrums.

Mike opened his door and called up. "What the hell is going on?"

I leaned over the railing. "It's the girl upstairs again."

He didn't answer me but called up the stairwell. "Oi! Shut up, kid."

It made no difference. I opened my door and went in, and as I did the bassline upstairs started. It felt like the walls were vibrating.

*

I called a dentist that Rachel had recommended. "He's gentle," she had said, giving me a black card. "And he works after five on Thursdays."

I booked an appointment and sat in his waiting room and read a tatty magazine.

There was an article on how wonderful it would be if women ruled the world, sandwiched between an advert for eyeliner and a double-page spread showing all the different outfits you could create with a black pencil skirt.

When I was a kid I always thought that as I got older I'd get naturally more fashionable, but it had never happened. Fashion was just full of rules that I didn't understand, so when I went shopping I was lost when it came to choosing one thing over another.

The dentist was called Dr Bhatti and he smiled at me warmly, though he didn't shake my hand. He already had his gloves on, and watched me climb onto his chair before he swung a light over my head.

I closed my eyes to avoid the glare.

"Not scared, are you?" he asked.

"No."

"So, any aches?"

"Yes. First it was one side, then the other, now both. Wisdom teeth, I think."

I could hear the plastic wheels of his stool rolling over the lino. "Open wide."

I did and he started probing my teeth with his foul-tasting gloves.

"You a student?"

"Ah." (No.)

"But you were?"

"Ah." (Yes.)

"Should have got your teeth done then. It would have been free."

He started saying numbers to his assistant.

After he was done I sat up.

"I understand you're in pain," he said, "but I'm very reluctant to take them out, very reluctant. Not impacted. Keep an eye on them. Come back."

He pulled off his glove and held out his hand for me to shake.

*

The papers announced a credit crunch, an economic recession. I saw the newspaper headline on some other commuter's paper. *The Beginning of the End.*

We were inundated with calls.

The phone had always been busier than I wanted it to be, but for a few months it had been steadily getting worse. The customer service post file contained items that were still unanswered from three months ago and Rachel's filing was over three feet high, but there was no question of her being able to do it.

Now, the phone rang at least once a minute so all day I got nothing done, and customer service fared no better.

I wondered if Big Nathan was pleased with the situation. He certainly must have felt like he was getting his money's worth out of us.

I thought of him telling me in the interview that my telephone would barely ring and I wondered if I could take him to an employment tribunal for misrepresentation.

I went over to see Ian, taking Shaun's chunk of filing with me. "Do you really need me to do this filing? Some of it is pretty old."

He leaned back in his chair and took it off me, flicking through it briefly. "It's not even in date order."

"No, this is the thing, I'll have to make it alphabetical and then date it."

"How long will it take you?"

"An afternoon, I should think. But I'll never get anything done with the phone the way it is, and the agreements are piling up, too."

Ian rubbed his chin. "Well, it's got to be done, I'm afraid. There's no way around it. But it's not a priority, so leave it for now."

"Okay."

That evening at the flats I heard a woman's shouts echoing round the corridor. At first I thought it was the mother upstairs again, but then I realised it was Mini Mum. I stood in the hallway, listening. Mini Man must have been outside their flat door.

"Fuck off! Just fuck off, you selfish bastard!"

"Oh, yeah, I'm fucking selfish. Who's gonna pay your fucking bills? Gas? Electricity? Food?"

I could hear Jessica grizzling.

"We don't need you, we don't want you, so just *fuck off.*"

"I fucking will, then. Let me get my stuff."

I heard footsteps and the door shutting.

I went back to the kitchen to check on my dinner, and five minutes later I heard a door slam in the corridor and then saw Mini Man striding across the courtyard. His jeans looked peach and I was surprised until I realised they were engrained with plaster dust and paint.

He opened up his van and I thought he was going to throw his stuff in and drive off in that, but he emerged with the Mini's roof and started fitting it. Mini Mum came out, with Jessica, who was still crying and trailing a blanket.

She didn't seem to move any slower for being pregnant, and leaned into the van's open door, pulling out a sledgehammer. Before Mini Man could get round to stop her, it'd gone through the Mini's back window. He put up his hands and held the back of his head.

She got the door, and then moved round to the bonnet.

"This is for your fucking daughter." And she hit it, over and over again.

I stopped watching. It felt intrusive. I wanted to tell the Traffic Warden and looked at my phone for a long time.

I didn't call him.

When I got up the next day, I noticed that my good bra had turned grey-pink, the colour of strawberry yoghurt. I didn't think it was that old, but as I was eating my cereal over the sink I thought back and couldn't remember the last time I'd bought one.

I could see out of the kitchen window that the Mini had no windscreen, and the driver's door and roof had big caves in them.

The van was gone.

*

"Good afternoon, you're through to reception, how can I help?"

A voice like butter. "Hello. How are you?"

I leaned back in my chair. "Oh, hello, Julia. I'm fine, thanks. How are you?"

"Not bad. Hoping these clouds break soon. Think we all need a bit of sun, don't you?"

"Absolutely."

"Are you going on holiday this summer?"

"Me? Doubtful. Are you?"

"Well, Roy and I are going to Spain."

"Roy?"

"Yes, my husband. He comes to the office sometimes – you must've seen him."

I couldn't think of any Roy. "I expect so."

"Anyway, is Nathan there?"

I checked. "He's on the phone. Do you want me to tell him to call you back?"

"If you don't mind."

"Of course not. He has your number, right?"

I could hear a smile in her voice. "Yes, I should hope so."

When I went to do submission, Mary was peeling another orange.

"On a health kick?"

"Something like that. It's hard with all these Easter eggs round the shops, though."

"I bet. Easter egg chocolate is the nicest chocolate there is." I took a blank submission form from the tray and started filling it in. "Can I ask you something?"

"Of course you can."

"Who *is* Julia?"

"Julia?"

"Yeah. She rings up sometimes, and asks for Big Nathan."

"She's his mum." The orange released this vapour into the air as she peeled it.

"Really? I thought she worked in the other office."

"She does. She works with RTW."

"Who is RTW?"

Ian laughed. "Cor, how long have you been working here?"

Mary flapped her hand at Ian to shut him up. "RTW is Roy Thomas Whittaker. Nathan's dad."

"Oh."

"Yeah."

"That has been quite a big mystery to me."

"You donkey," Ian said.

"Well," Mary said, passing me a segment of orange. "Now you know."

I won both ICS and CRS submission. "Let's see the graph, then."

Young Nathan turned his monitor round.

I pointed to the red bar. "Is that me? I'm six ahead."

"Yeah. The graph makes it look more than it is."

"Whatever."

"It's true, look at the scale."

"That's almost an insurmountable lead."

"It's not."

"*Almost*. You'd have to win three full days just to get level."

"It's not insurmountable."

"Loser."

"Not insurmountable."

I went over to Big Nathan's desk to hand him the submission reports. "I have a question." I said it quickly, before I could stop myself.

He smiled and swivelled round so he faced me straight on. "Yes?"

"I was wondering if it'd be possible for me to go on lunch at the same time as everyone else. It's not a big deal or anything, but all I can tell people who ring up between one and two is that I can't help them and they have to ring back."

"Okay."

"Really?"

"Yeah. I'll get Mark to rig your line up to the answerphone, so it'll go on with everyone else's at one."

I smiled. "Thanks."

*

That evening, I noticed the Venus fly trap had produced a flower. It had grown on a green stick coming out of the middle, and had off-white, ragged petals.

It had never occurred to me that it would produce a flower.

So much energy had it taken that the mouths had started to look a little sad. I wished that I had set up a camera on time delay, so that now I could put the pictures together and watch the mouths growing and opening and snapping, before turning black and curling up and disintegrating.

It had surprised me how little I minded being alone.

I kept thinking that I was passing through a phase, and one day I'd revert to being like I was before, but there was no sign of it. The whole time I'd been with the Traffic Warden, being alone had terrified me, but now it just *was*.

There was no one to complain or monitor my actions, so I could read as late as I wanted, and often stayed up until four in the morning. If I felt like having a few drinks, I did; if I felt like staying in bed until four in the afternoon, then I did; if I felt like watching hours of TV or playing music loud, then I did.

On Friday evening I walked to the offie at the end of our road.

The owner of the shop looked like a Bengali version of Danny DeVito and was one of those shopkeepers who had been there a long time and knew everyone in the vicinity. He was stacking cans of Carling in the fridge when I got there.

"Hello," I said. "How are you?"

"Yes, very well, thank you."

"Working late?"

"Yes, finish late, but start late. Evenings go quick, you know?" He went and stood behind the register and waited for me to make my selections. I couldn't bear the idea of people waiting for me, though he did look used to it.

"How was your day?" he asked.

"Yeah, it was okay," I said. "That Friday feeling, you know." I thought about telling him about the office, but stopped myself as I couldn't think what to say.

"Weather will be good tomorrow."

"You reckon? I've been thinking that for months."

"Sky is red."

As I stepped outside, I saw that he was right: the sky was streaked pink and orange. It was the first good sunset I'd seen in ages.

I listened to the clink of the bottles in the bag. I'd always loved that sound. My dad used to take me to the offie with him when I was a kid and I would look at all those bottles of dark liquid lined up like soldiers, waiting for him to decide, and wonder what the difference could possibly be amongst them. He'd always buy my mum a walnut whip and since I was never allowed one, it seemed the most exotic thing in the world to me.

I watched a vapour trail mark the sky, though I couldn't see the aeroplane.

The next day I woke up sweating. I got out of bed and into the shower, and something felt different but I didn't work out what until I opened the blind in the bedroom. I could see the sun.

*

The Traffic Warden's mother rang me as I was making dinner on the Sunday night.

"I just wanted to say I was sorry," she said. "About you two."

I stirred the sauce I was making. "Yeah. So am I." My voice cracked.

"We were – we *are* very fond of you. Both of us. We'll miss you."

"Yeah, me too." I didn't know what to say, or even if I could. "I am sad. But we don't want the same things in life any more."

"That's exactly what he said."

There was a long pause. I listened to my sauce bubbling away.

"Well, I'll let you get on. I just wanted to make sure you're okay."

"That's very sweet of you."

When she hung up, I stood by the cooker and cried while my dinner burnt to the bottom of the pan.

*

On Monday, work was sweltering. All the fans in the office buzzed and turned their faces like owls surveying us. We had opened all the windows as far as possible, but shut all the blinds and turned the lights off to reduce glare from the monitors.

I was going to the park with Rachel at lunchtime. When we stepped outside, I asked, "Do you remember the first time we came out here?"

"No."

"You twirled around and asked me what the fuck I was doing here. That was almost a year ago, and I still don't know."

"Nor me. When are we getting our PRs?"

"I don't know. Soon, I guess. Anyway. How's Amy?"

"She's okay. I bought her this book that's meant to help explain death to kids. It's called *Goodbye Mousie*, so you can imagine what it's like."

"Has it been helpful?"

"In short, no. She has surmised that we are getting a mouse."

I laughed. "Sorry."

"No, it is funny. Bless her. I don't know what I'd do without her, sometimes."

"You'd come and get drunk with me."

"Yeah! Anyway, how are you?"

"I'm okay."

She waved a wasp away. "Really?"

"Well, you know."

"Yeah."

"Ooh, guess what?"

"What?"

"Kim's coming back."

"I wondered when that was going to happen."

I was disappointed at her complete lack of surprise. "Really? I didn't think she would ever, let alone before her maternity leave finishes. Lexi's not even four months old. And Kim's hardly a career woman – I mean, what did she even ever do at Weblands but odd jobs?"

"It's not that. That's nothing to do with it. When you're pregnant, everyone makes a big fuss over you, but once you have the baby, you're shoved aside. Your life becomes about the baby, and that means your family, your friends, too. No one is remotely interested in you. You are *nothing*."

I put my hand on my stomach and thought of the son I hadn't had yet. I could still see him, staring at me through the bars of the cot. "Did that happen to you?"

"Yes. But I didn't mind. Kim would."

"I think I would, too."

"You think you will, but you won't. Nothing is the same when you have babies. *Everything* changes."

"I know, but... to feel like *nothing* is a little dramatic, do you not think?"

"It's a biological reaction." She held up her hands like blinkers. "Everything is about the baby."

"Yes, but I mean to be any use as a carer you have to take some care of yourself as well."

"Yeah, sure. But it's the all-time minimum. I barely brushed my hair for a year after having Amy."

I thought of when I'd gone round to see her, and perhaps she did too.

"Anyway, I'm not the least bit surprised about Kim," she said. "Not the least bit."

"I wonder if she'll start doing submission again. How pathetic is this, but I hope not. I quite like it."

Rachel held out a carrier bag and I put a foil ball and a banana skin in it.

"Well, whatever she does, she won't be queen bee any more," she said. We got up and checked each other's arses.

"Queen bee?" I asked.

"Yeah."

"Is this another of your weird telepathy things?"

"No, no, it's the dominant female force in the office. You know what I mean."

"What? There's no queen bee at Weblands."

"Of course there is."

"Well, who is it now, then?"

"You."

*

Another afternoon, another submission. I put the phone on answer as it was so busy.

"So have you heard from Kim? Do you know when she's coming back?" I asked Mary.

"End of next week, I should think."

"Really? That soon?"

Mary lowered her voice. "She must miss all the male

243

attention."

I was surprised to hear her insult Kim, since I had thought I was the only one who found her annoying. "What male attention?"

"Oh, you know, Kyle, Nick, Mark – she flirted with them all. And poor Young Nathan here certainly knew more about pregnancy than he ever needed to."

I turned to him and he nodded, and then reached into his drawer and pulled out a packet of humbugs, putting them in the middle of the desks.

"Thanks," I said, taking one and then turning to Mary. "What will she be doing? Do you know?"

She took a humbug too, and unwrapped it. "I'm not sure. Plenty of work to go round, though, isn't there?"

"Certainly is." I nodded slowly and got on with the submission.

"You're not going to like this," I said.

"What?"

"I've won both submissions."

Young Nathan got up and came round to check my screen.

"What are you checking it for? I could have been lying to you every other day since we began."

"Today is important."

"Why?"

He didn't answer, just scrutinised the screen.

"It's not the end of April yet."

He went back round to his desk, tapped something into his computer, and then winced.

"What is it?"

His voice was low and quiet. "It's insurmountable."

I cupped my ear towards him. "Say that again."

"Loser."

"Ooh, I think the word you're looking for is *winner*."

Ian was smirking.

Mary reached into her top drawer for an orange. "Thing is, what are you going to do now it's over?"

I looked at Young Nathan.

"We'll just have to think of a new game."

*

My phone rang.

It was Big Nathan.

I picked it up. "Hello."

"Are you ready?"

"Yes."

"Come on, then."

He stood up and so did I, and I followed him out of the office and downstairs to the room where I had had my interview.

The weather was hot and my clothes were stifling and prickly, like electricity.

I sat on one side of the office, and he sat on the other. He had a pad and pencil. I had nothing.

"So. This is your performance review."

"Yes."

He consulted his pad. "Well, I'm very happy with your work. You're punctual. Your input numbers are… excellent."

I nodded. "Good."

"And I know all about your telephone manner. How have you found the workload since Shaun… left?"

I felt I should be honest. "Almost unchanged."

"Well, you'll be pleased to know that you will be assisted again soon, hopefully more effectively this time. But if the workload becomes too much at any point before then, you must let me know. How do you see yourself progressing?"

"Progressing?"

"Yes. As I said to you at the start, promotion is flexible here."

"That's good." The truth was I didn't know enough about what anyone else actually did to want their job. They all seemed much the same to me. Everyone sat at a computer, everyone spoke on the phone, everyone moaned about refilling the photocopier with paper.

"So you enjoy your job, then?"

I held his gaze for a second. I wanted to see my life flash before my eyes. "Yes."

He smiled. "Pleased to hear it."

"I have one question, though."

"Yes."

"Shaun told me you employed him to liven up the office."

Big Nathan sort of smirked. "Ye-s…"

"Well, why did you employ me?"

There was a strange and heavy silence.

"I do know why I employed you, actually. You seemed interesting."

"Really?"

"Yes."

"That's it?"

"Yeah."

We got up together and shook hands, and as we did I caught a glimpse of his pad.

It was blank.

*

The minute I stepped into the office, I knew she was back.

She was leaning against Young Nathan's desk and had her back to the door, so she didn't see me.

"Guess who's coming to sit with you…"

I looked up to see her slipping into the seat opposite me, empty since Shaun's departure.

"Hi," she said. She was smiling.

"Hi."

"How's it been? Same old, same old?"

"More or less. How's you? And Lexi?"

"Oh, she's a terror. I do not wanna talk about babies, or baby things, ever again." She put her hands together and balanced her chin on them. "So. What do you want me to do?"

I sighed and slowly reached under the desk. "Well, I do have some transmittal forms that need filing."

*

When I got home, upstairs had *Sweet Child o' Mine* blasting out.

I started doing the washing-up and noticed that the smashed-up Mini had gone from its spot.

I went to the front room, opened the window and lit a cigarette. Upstairs seemed to have *Sweet Child o' Mine* on repeat. I sat in the deckchair, listening to the guitar. I used to love that song, before I went to university and realised it was as much a certainty as VodBull for a pound at every student night, along with Bryan Adams and the Proclaimers.

The song finished, and then started again.

Before I could bottle it, I left my cigarette in the ashtray and found myself outside the door of flat nine.

Dusty answered the door. He was wearing the same grey hoodie that I'd first seen him in.

I had no idea what to say.

247

"Hello," he said.

I could hear people laughing behind him. "Hi. Sorry to come up here, but the music's a bit loud."

"Oh, is it? Sorry. We'll turn it down, no worries."

I could still hear *Sweet Child o' Mine* over his shoulder. "Are you just playing one song on repeat?"

"Well, sort of – we're playing *Guitar Hero*, and Jason's trying to beat my score."

"*Guitar Hero*?"

"Yeah. On the Xbox. Wanna join?"

I smiled. "No, thanks."

*

Rachel put her phone down. "Right, that's it. I'm going to file."

"Are you feeling okay?"

"Yeah." She smiled. "I think I'm getting that syndrome where your muscles are in the same position for too long."

"I know what you mean."

Kim had spent her first morning filing the transmittal forms, and more than that; she'd actually gone through the fles and corrected, as far as I knew, all of Shaun's mistakes. The fact that this job was now done made me feel strangely at peace.

She input roughly as fast as me, which meant we were whipping through the stack at quite a rate.

I reached into my drawer, and put a bag of sweets in the middle of our desks. "Humbug?"

"I'm never going to lose my excess like this," she said.

"Ah, life's too short."

"Perhaps." She took one, and I could hear it clicking against her teeth.

I watched Rob, manager of debt collection, swing lazily back and forth on his chair, throwing a ball of Blu-Tack between his hands. He was saying stuff I'd heard him say before, as although he didn't have a script there were certain excuses people came up with over and over again.

I heard him say, "Well, I *have* listened to you. But you're not listening to me," a decibel above the usual, and I felt the ears of the office prick up.

"No, no, I'm sorry but that's not the case at all… You signed the agreement, so it's up to you to pay it… I can't comment on that because I wasn't there… No, it's not a matter of convenience, Mr Tunstall. Actually, it's not very convenient for me to ring you up – will you listen to me, please? I've listened to you, now listen to me… No, that's completely irrelevant… No… I'm not the police…" I saw Ian spin his chair in Rob's direction, and I caught his eye. "Mr Tunstall… Mr Tunstall… No, I'm not al-Quaeda." He banged the phone down. "Fucking twat."

The office tittered with laughter, even Ruth.

"It's certainly an idea for expansion," Big Nathan said. "Suicide bombing."

Kim got up. "Right. Post time, I think."

"Are you sure you don't mind doing it?"

"No, not at all. Just remind me quickly, is it the photocopies I'm sending or the originals?"

I was surprised she asked, since she'd spent all those years filing the original transmittals. "Photocopies."

Rachel and I went to the park at lunch. It was hot, and we lay on the crispy sun-baked grass on our backs.

"So how's it working out with Kim?"

"Pretty good, actually. She seems a little more… I don't know…

249

amenable?"

"She does a bit."

"The weird thing is, though, she's only been away for a few months and she's forgotten *everything*. I mean really basic stuff."

"Don't be too hard on her. You forget everything when you have a baby."

"Really?"

"Yep."

I propped myself on one elbow and shielded my eyes from the sun. "Jeez, I'm glad it's not up to you to market procreation."

"How do you mean?"

"Have a baby and become a stupid nobody."

"Oh, no, not at all. But I don't want to lie about the way it was for me. There are so many stories around childbirth, so much folklore. But you only know it when it happens to you."

"And not a moment before."

We lay in silence.

I felt funny lying there in my stuffy office clothes. I had the urge to peel them all off and run around on the grass. There is a real mental disorder that occurs only in some Eskimo tribes, where the main symptom is people tearing off their clothes and running into the snow and ice. It makes sense that they would consider this the height of craziness; in that environment, where survival is about staying warm, it's what you must never do.

"Do you think it's mad to be unhappy when you're basically living in luxury?"

She didn't think, even for a second. "No."

"Why not?"

"Well, depends what you mean by luxury."

"I mean it in a basic way. It's not like we all live in gold houses. But we all have a roof over our head and food and clothes and stuff."

"But everyone has that, so it's not a luxury."

"But everything you have is something you could lose tomorrow."

I looked into her eyes and I knew she was thinking of her dad.

"I know," she said.

I wondered what the Traffic Warden was doing. Probably sitting in a car somewhere, eating a pasty. Or smoking. He never minded smoking on hot days, but I did. It tasted strange, wrong somehow.

As if Rachel had read my mind she sat up and lit up a fag. "Want one?"

"No, I'm okay, thanks."

"You're thinking about him."

"Yeah."

"And?"

"What if I've chopped my right arm off just to prove I can live without it?"

"What if the sky falls?"

I looked up, into the endless blue, and lay down again.

"Are you unhappy?" she asked.

I felt the heat of the air soaking into my skin. "No."

*

I didn't have much in the fridge but I did have a packet of sausages, so I started to fry them up. I didn't put any music on like I used to, but listened to them crackling in the pan. I was cutting up some peppers and thinking how beautiful the cross-section was when I heard the key in the door.

I stood in the hallway with the knife still in my hand, and there he was. He looked different, like a slightly discoloured version of a painting that I knew very well.

"Hello, Belly."

"You're back."

"Yeah."

"Do you need a hand?"

I followed him down the stairs and out to the car, and he handed me the Xbox.

"Be careful with that, now."

"What, that's all you're giving me? I can take something else on top."

He pulled out a bin liner full of clothes and straightened up. "I don't want anything on top of it."

I rolled my eyes. "Okay, well, I'm not helping any more."

He brought the rest of the stuff in and then stood in the kitchen while I finished making dinner, just so he could talk to me. It was something I wished he'd done when we'd been together.

"So, how have you been?" I asked.

"Okay. You?"

"Yeah. Good, thanks." I didn't know what else to say. "Pretty, pretty, pretty good."

He took out a vacuum pack of garlic sausage slices from a Tesco bag he'd brought in with him.

"Did you go to your mum's?"

"No, I went to my other girlfriend's."

"Oh, I forgot how hilarious you were." I slid some discs of courgette into the mix. "Listen, I don't know if I thought we were forever…" I stirred the sauce for a minute, rolling the spoon in it. "I don't even know if I believe in that, but I never thought it would be like this."

"Yeah."

I put the spoon down and turned to him, my arms folded. "I don't take back anything I said. But I'm still sorry."

He folded another slice of sausage into his mouth. "Well, it's not as if one of us cheated. That's something. At least we were honest."

I reached out for a slice of sausage and he pulled the pack away. Usually we would have wrestled in our socks like kids until I got one, but then he just gave it to me. It felt spicy and flat in my mouth.

"I had this weird dream last night," he said.

I didn't think he'd ever told me about a single one of his dreams. "What was it about?"

"I had seven cats. In a big house. And they kept escaping. And I couldn't get them back."

"Kind of prophetic, huh?"

"What do you mean?"

"Never mind." The motor in the fridge stopped running and the kitchen fell completely silent. "I do have a very important question, though." I pushed the window open. The sky was pink. "Who gets the sandwich toaster?"

"You can have it."

"One good thing to come out of us, then."

He smiled and so did I. There was only the sound of the dinner bubbling away and him chewing salami.

"What will you do?" he asked.

"Move to London," I said.

"I don't need to ask if you'll be okay, do I?"

"No."

He saw me looking at the last salami slice in the pack and handed it to me with his bare fingers.

"Thanks."

Acknowledgements

There are a lot of people I'd like to thank but none more so than Dan Holloway, who was the earliest champion of this book and a great ally, and also Clive Birnie, who found, read and liked the novel enough to want to publish it, and then put tireless efforts into the production and distribution.

Massive thanks to John Mahood for his insight into putting a cover together and for never being too busy to humour my ideas, and also fabulous copyeditor Harriet Evans.

Thanks to the two best teachers I had: Mary Smith, who brought home the reality of bad writing by lying on the floor in the middle of an English lesson, and Scarlett Thomas, who told me I should write a novel in the first place.

I couldn't really do anything without these guys, who have all been there with encouragement, ideas and merlot... thanks Chanelle, Sarah, Laura, Lauren, Kay, Peter and Liz.

And lastly, thanks to my dad for telling me to "Just do what you love" when I was endlessly agonising over what degree subject to choose, and thank you, Mum, for everything.